About the

Jane Deans is retired from her teaching career and lives with her husband in Dorset. Having written sporadically throughout her teaching life, since retirement she has written in earnest, producing a wide range of work including short stories, a novel, *The Year of Familiar Strangers*, and a regular travel blog, Graceless Ageing (gracelessageing.wordpress.com).

She has collaborated in the running of a writing group, The Spokes, since 2014 and is a voracious reader, particularly of quality contemporary fiction. She travels extensively for much of the year, spending weeks with her husband in a camper van, researching and writing in whichever location they find themselves. She is also a keen gardener and a passionate supporter of environmental causes.

THE CONWAYS AT EARTHSEND

Jane Deans

THE CONWAYS AT EARTHSEND

Vanguard Press

A CIP catalogue record for this title is
available from the British Library.

ISBN 978 1 784659 61 5

*Vanguard Press is an imprint of
Pegasus Elliot MacKenzie Publishers Ltd.*
www.pegasuspublishers.com

First Published in 2021

**Vanguard Press
Sheraton House Castle Park
Cambridge England**

Printed & Bound in Great Britain

Dedication

For my supportive daughter and my
long-suffering husband.

Acknowledgements

Thanks to all at Pegasus. Thank you to my daughter, Amy, for her support, encouragement and suggestions throughout the project. Thanks also to fellow writer, Ian Muir, for his advice during our editorial swap.

Lastly thanks to my wonderful writing group, The Spokes, who maintain a love and pleasure for the written word for its own sake.

CONTENTS

The Kill

The storm gathers for four days before keeping its promise, loosening a cacophony of thunder and howling winds and a deluge.

In the chaos, vessels buck and rage against their moorings. Dwellings shudder and creak in their weaknesses. People stay in, cowering, sheltering, from whatever damage ensues. The hillside above the village becomes a furious torrent; a tumbling waterfall then a landslide as the soil gives way and a gushing brown channel of mud races down carrying soil, rocks, roots and debris.

In the sky, intermittent flashes expose the silhouettes of the towering turbines across the hilltop, skeletal against jagged forks of lightning. Along the tunnels, tattered edges of white plastic flap like so much unruly laundry, beginning with a border here, a corner there, then ripping in abandoned strips. Wind and water race into the gaping chasms they've made, desecrating all inside.

A tall eye on a stalk swivels in a slow revolution, water cascading from its top as it detects warmth and movement. A figure darts into view, swathed in a cape and hood, head first bent then upturned, reaching up to catch a flap of torn fabric, grasping, pinning down.

Below, in the darkness and the ferment, an unlit vehicle approaches, creeping its way up along the track, lashed by the driving volley, buffeted by the cyclonic gusts and beset by loose rocks hurling themselves against its sides and beneath the sturdy, all-terrain wheels, two pale faces inside leaning forwards, straining for a view of the upward track as it curls around the hill, black water streaming across their route before hurtling down towards the river mouth.

Unknowing, the caped figure works on, lashed by the storm, pegging, weighing down, battening as the grey truck draws closer, invisible in the curtains of rain and silent in the screaming wind as it whips and sings around the tunnels.

The truck halts beyond the outer fence, disregarded by the frantic worker. More bolts of lightning split the sky illuminating vast structures shifting, protesting under the onslaught and giving brief insights into the hopelessness of the task; more and more material wrenching free to flap like hapless sails in a shipwreck.

Now the passenger is clambering out, reaching back inside for tools, hunched against the elements, chancing the small pinpoint of a flashlight. A blaze of lightning bursts over the razor wire as he inserts first one clip then another before applying bolt cutters. In a few moments a gap appears wide enough for the truck to pass through.

The caped one has disappeared up along the side of

the polytunnel doing what he can, saving, preserving.

The truck pulls through into the security channel ready for the cutting process to be repeated on the other, inner fence and it rolls through the second breach. The driver emerges, fighting his way to the rear of the vehicle and wrenching the tailgate open before joining his companion. They move quickly into a breach in a tunnel, emerging with cartons, battered, fighting the gusts as they place their booty into the truck bed, returning for more, their arms piled with boxes four high, the shorter, slighter of the two staggering sideways as the bulkier and taller figure grips his arm. He indicates they should move on to the next tunnel as his partner hesitates. He stores his boxes then lifts his hand in protest. *'Enough! Let's go!'* But the other is off into the neighbouring cavern, reappearing with another load, water coursing down his face and beard. Then in an instant both figures freeze, one laden with cartons, the other by the truck's open tailgate as the dark shape of a dog appears in front of them, a black shadow outlined by lightning flashes, long head low, sodden fur raised up in a barb of wet spikes along its back. Its ears are flat alongside its head and its open mouth a snarling saw of serrated teeth, white razor points dripping drool, slavering, growl unheard in the screech of the gale.

Bulky makes a gradual half turn to Slight, the indication clear. *'Get in the truck!'* Slight stands fast. The dog raises its head, mouth open, tensing to spring. Bulky lifts the cartons high and hurls them in the beast's direction before jumping sideways into the open aperture of the cab. The dog leaps towards him as the door closes on its head, its jaws fastened tight upon Bulky's arm. He works in a frantic bid to free it, smashing the door repeatedly with his right hand until it withdraws, then slamming it shut. One in, one out. Slight still stands amongst the crates, rooted.

The dog, bloodied and enraged, barks his frustration into the wind — a harsh, jarring yowl then turning as its attention is drawn by another, a pale form running towards the vehicle. The dog leaps. The caped figure falls backwards, a black shadowy parasite attached to him as he is hurled on to the sodden ground in a mire of mud, water, man, animal and now blood. His body jerks like a dancing marionette as his screams are whisked away into the whirling gusts and the plunging deluge. Slight springs for the van, dropping the boxes to spill into the wet mud as two more dogs loom up into the narrow beam, loping towards their pack-mate. Cape man's arms and legs flay, his hands upon his face tugged away by more biting, grabbing jaws. They tear at his limbs, fabric giving way to flesh, flesh to blood and bone, exposed in each bright flare of lightning. The two inside the truck stare out as his screams subside, draining away in the steady flow of blood from the open gash that was his throat.

Slight vomits into the truck floor as Bulky shouts, yelling at him to '*Get and Drive!*' After a moment the truck begins to reverse between the razor ends, back through the gap, out of the security channel, away from the carnage.

Shots explode above the thunder. The writhing, seething mass of snarling bodies becomes still. A fourth figure runs towards the mangled heap, rifle in hand as he drops to his knees amongst the bloody, visceral mess to heave away the inert bodies of the dogs. He leans down, taking the torn and bloody corpse in his arms, stroking the matted hair and crying unheard in the still raging storm as the water continues to fall, washing red life away to the ground in a dark rivulet that mingles with the torrent of mud, earth and slime on their way down the mountainside.

Three months earlier…

Laura

Above all, it was birdsong she missed. You could become accustomed to relentless drumming on the slate roof, the incessant, rhythmic drip from the overhanging eaves on to the flagstone paths below and the various percussive assaults on the windows ranging from intermittent pattering to fully-blown pounding. But she longed for periods of silence, punctuated only by the joyful songs of small, wild birds proclaiming their delight in being alive. It was rare, during a prolonged spell such as this, to even spot a bird, let alone to hear one. They were there in the borders of the garden, sheltering like refugees, detectable only in the momentary shake of a wet branch or a dark blur in pursuit of an elusive bug; never perched audaciously, plumped up in public view and performing an assertive claim to property rights. Laura scrutinised the sturdy boughs of the apple tree, once a favourite perch of wild birds, but could detect no movement amongst the remaining blossom except for repeated jerking from the pummelling of raindrops. Around the top of the tree there were vestiges of an old tree house she and her sister Cath had played in as children, built by their father. A few years ago, when Holly was about six, he'd offered to resurrect it for her to use, but there never seemed to be a long enough dry period for the work to be undertaken; then never a sustained interval of sunshine for the completion of such a project to be enjoyed, so the last, few remaining, rotting planks clung around the trunk at head height, green with moss and algae, redundant.

Holly was sitting in her favourite spot on the broad window seat, knees propped up, engrossed in the book Hugh had given her. She held it with care, cradling it as the precious object it had become, turning each page in a slow, reverent motion, peering with the utmost concentration at the illustrations, sliding a finger softly across the thick, yellowing paper and leaning forwards to sniff the aroma of ancient ink and creamy vellum. Laura crossed the living room to sit by her daughter, her back to the latticed window, where rivulets streamed down in a madcap race to reach the bottom of each pane and pool on the stone sill outside. She watched the girl's rapt expression, her dark lashes stark on her pale cheeks as she scrutinised the picture and ran her fingertips down the page's uneven, deckle edging.

"Did Granddad give you another book?"

The girl lifted it from her lap to display the cover; dark brown with a pale oval in the centre displaying the title: 'The Snow Lamb' and a small print — a winter landscape with a background of snow-clad pine trees surrounding a field in which a small lamb was portrayed, its eyes wide with fear, its mouth open in a frightened bleat. Laura remembered it, remembered having it read to her on successive bedtimes, tucked into bed in the tiny bedroom in the eaves now occupied by her daughter. Holly looked up.

"I wish we had snow. I'd love to know what it was like. Granddad used to play in the snow when he was a child, he told me. It must have been fun!"

Laura nodded, smiling at her daughter and tucking a lock of unruly, red-gold hair behind the child's ear. "He used to tell us about it, too. Granddad had a toboggan to ride on. He'd pull it up Gethyn Hill on a rope then he'd get his brother to sit on the front and he'd have to shove off and jump on before it got going. He'd usually fall off at the bottom, but it did no harm on the soft snow. He'd just get up and go back up for another go." She broke off, thinking of her own sister, Cath, of how close they'd been as young children and how things had changed with the onset of adolescence; the differences in their personalities more marked as the years passed.

"Do you think it was cold, the snow?" Holly's eyes shone, excited at the image. Laura thought they couldn't be more different, her two children; a dark, slim, wiry boy and a tall, auburn-haired and athletic girl. Holly took after her father, who was a red-haired giant of a man.

"Oh, it was cold, but they never minded that! It was too much fun to worry about the cold. Did you have any homework today?"

Holly nodded. "Mrs Philips wants us to get ready for the VT tomorrow by choosing an area we want to research and preparing some questions. After the tour we'll have to make a presentation of what we've learned."

"Have you checked the headset? You don't want anything to go wrong halfway through the tour, do you? You could try it out on one of Dad's demo films."

Her daughter shrugged, pouting.

"I wish we could go on real trips, you know, like Granddad used to. It must have been fantastic, getting on a big vehicle altogether and travelling, really *travelling,* to an actual place; to a museum or to an ancient monument, sitting next to your friend, having sandwiches together, getting to walk around, touch things." Laura stroked her daughter's hair. She knew Holly loved listening to Granddad Hugh's stories but they sometimes made her dissatisfied with life.

Her own early childhood had been so different from Holly's. There had always been pets; a fat tabby cat that liked to sleep the day away in a patch of sunshine on her bed, a soft, black Labrador called Dixie that she and Cath would take for walks along the river. He would dive in after sticks and never want to leave the water. He'd be in his element now, she thought; there was water everywhere, more than they knew what to do with.

They were interrupted by an urgent buzz.

"Go ahead, PAM," said Laura.

"There is a message from Josh, Laura." PAM's mellifluous, cultured tone sounded throughout the stone cottage, accompanied by the flashing pinpoint of green light on the ceiling speaker.

"Go on PAM."

"Josh will not be in for another two hours, at least. He has to attend to a malfunction in a drainage tube outside tunnel thirteen. He says to carry on with dinner and not to wait for him. He is hoping to be back in time before Holly goes to bed."

"Right. OK. Thanks PAM."

It was odd, she thought, that they were always so polite to the Personal Address Messenger, as if she were a real human and not the automated information system they relied on. Perhaps one day she would assume human characteristics such as personality and emotions and take over the world. Laura smiled at the irony. PAM might make a better job of it than we humans have, she thought.

Holly moved the treasured book on to the seat and stood up.

"Can I suit up and go out to help Dad? He might be in earlier and we'd be able to eat dinner together." Her rosy face contorted with pleading then relaxed into a slump of disappointment as Laura shook her head.

"It would be getting dark before you got up to the tunnels, love. I know what a wonderful help you would be, but I can't risk you going up there by yourself. What if there was a slippage? Your father has had his hands full these last few weeks just containing the hillside above Lantern Howe. Farlow will be up there with him. You can help out here; take a tray in to Granddad in a bit. Your Granddad gets more out of seeing you than he does from the rest of us put together!"

It was only a year since her mother had been taken to rest. During the previous couple of years, Laura had begun to realise that the small alterations in her mother's behaviour signified a more insidious change in the form of dementia. At the beginning there were the nagging anxieties she'd begun to express over trivial matters. She had become agitated, fluttering like a trapped bird if Hugh went outside, if she mislaid an item or whenever PAM buzzed a message.

As time went on, she forgot routines like washing and dressing, needing to be coaxed like a small child into swapping her dressing gown for day clothes and later she habitually confused family members, calling Laura 'Mum' and Holly, Cath — Laura's sister's name. Although he continued to be her primary carer, her husband, Hugh, was himself no longer the sprightly hill farmer he used to be, rising at six in all weathers and striding out to see to livestock and crops with a minimum of assistance. Despite suffering from age related conditions such as arthritis and hearing loss, he insisted on taking care of his wife with little respite, except for whenever Laura could persuade him to take a break. She had often resorted to subterfuge, suggesting that Joshua might need an experienced eye to look over the cabbages in Tunnel four, or that Holly would appreciate some input to her homework. Hugh was rarely fooled yet he'd recognised the value of time off, even from his fragile, beloved wife, Ellen.

They had been lucky, Laura considered, to be in a situation where her mother had been supported at home amongst her own family, surrounded by those who loved and cared about her. Most families' loved ones would have been summoned to rest as soon as diagnosis was made. She had made use of regular check-ups via virtual diagnosis, persuading Ellen to sit for the web surround-sensor and perform the tasks that the v-doc set but had also been able to influence the results with small adjustments. Sometimes PAM had buzzed a message to her suggesting some new medication or technique, most of which she took up gladly. Then the v-doc decreed that her mother's time was up, devastating for everyone except the subject herself. The loss of her was still new and raw to them all, none more so than Hugh. Laura noticed he'd become distant lately and prone to long silences and losses of concentration.

PAM announced Josh's arrival at ten and he appeared a few minutes later, having removed and stored the cumbersome bio-suit in which he spent his working days. As he strode into the room his daughter flung herself at him, wrapping her arms around his waist, eliciting a wide grin from her father.

Joshua Conway was used to dipping his head to avoid bashing it on the low ceilings of the farmhouse.

Laura's husband was a large, vital man, tall and broad in stature, possessed of a confident, vibrant nature so that he filled any room wherever he went. Bio-cultivation was his passion, motivating him to succeed as much for a desire for scientific discovery and advances in addressing the world's needs as the more pragmatic requirements of looking after his dependents. One of the reasons Laura had fallen in love with him was that he considered himself fortunate to work in an area that fascinated him, addressed his altruistic tendencies and provided for his family.

He glanced up from Holly to meet his wife's pained expression.

"I'd have been in earlier, but I sent Farlow home at nine. I didn't want Ewa worrying about him in her condition. She doesn't have long to go, now. I'm starving though. What are we having?"

"It's chem-beef loaf. I hope it didn't dry out as it has been kept warm for a while. I didn't want to re heat it. Holly's had hers and she needs to get to bed right now. She has this tour thing tomorrow."

Josh reached down to his daughter, swinging her up in an effortless movement and manoeuvring her around to perch upon his back, where she clung, rosy and smiling.

"I'll be your carriage for tonight, my lady Holly," he said. "If you're comfortable we'll be off."

She broke into a peal of delighted laughter, arms clutched tight around his neck. "Where are you taking me?"

"Well, to the country of dreams of course; the land where anything is possible! And while we are travelling, I want to know all about this trip you are taking tomorrow — this educational visit."

Laura could still hear their chattering banter, muffled as they ascended the stairs. She served up the last two plates of dinner, pouring two glasses of wine to accompany it before pausing to gaze out at the rain and wonder where Ethan was and what he was doing.

When they had Ethan, Laura had assumed that he would grow up to take on responsibility for the bio-farm, just as she and Joshua had, but he'd shown less interest in matters of cultivation as he grew, turning instead to a burgeoning curiosity in the ways of water. He'd become fascinated, first by stories about pirates, then absorbed in shipping and boats, so that he began to make crude model craft for himself, aided by his grandfather, and experiment with sailing them outside. By the time Holly was born he'd determined that his future lay on the water. When he was only seventeen, he left to pursue a career in marine transport, a choice that had disappointed she and Joshua in the beginning but was now a source of pride for both of them.

Most evenings Laura and Joshua went in to see Hugh before he went to bed, knowing the old man appreciated being kept up to date with developments on the farm and recognising the old man's need for a diversion from the intense and sometimes heart-aching pressure of grieving for his wife.

"Late tonight then, Josh; drainage problem, Laura said."

Now eighty-four, though Hugh Evans was diminished in stature, a little bent over and hard of hearing, he embodied the term 'sprightly' in every way, taking a keen interest in the fortunes of the farm, the family, current affairs and environmental matters. However, whilst Josh and Laura knew and appreciated the value of his experience in running the farm, there was a limit to the extent to which he could advise now that science ruled the realm of cultivation. Laura came from an academic background of agro-research, choosing to apply her knowledge in the area of food production and had met Joshua whilst she was studying for a degree in sustainable agriculture.

The old man was sitting in his favourite chair, a relic from his own family life here in this same house, before the annexe had been built. The sturdy, sixteenth century, stone farmhouse with its slate roof had been constructed to withstand the worst conditions the British climate could subject it to, but Laura was often forced to reflect that no one at that time could have forecast what was to come, here and now, in the twenty-first century; or that humankind would have been responsible, somehow, for bringing this change upon itself.

Hugh had been listening to orchestral music, a favourite activity in the evenings and one that soothed him. These days his thoughts were often occupied by his daughter, Cath, whose whereabouts remained a mystery since she'd fled the family home as a teenager. Now he asked PAM to turn the music off as his daughter and son-in-law sat opposite with a last tot of whisky, to describe the day's events.

Earthsend

The two figures, mother and daughter, dressed in their glowing, green-yellow bio-suits and spiked galoshes wound their way along the hillside path towards the tunnels. Above them, over Gethyn Hill, the towering turbines' vast blades turned, emitting their continuous, whining hum; a whistling wind in a stark white, giant forest.

As they walked, Holly and Laura inspected the slope above them for signs of slip, but this year's netting appeared to be holding. Below, on the downhill side, there were fresh deposits of mud and rocks from a recent slide, indicating that the track might need additional support in the next few weeks.

They rounded the bend and the tunnel field came into view. From here at the corner the scene before them looked as if the entire landscape had been wrapped up in neat, white, cylindrical parcels and laid in rows as far as the eye could see. Far away in the distance the dark, green fringe of Longhope Forest marked the border of the property, dividing it from the neighbouring bio-fuel plant, 'Greenergy', but was reduced, these days, mainly to conifers since the rapid decline of deciduous trees during the last hundred years.

Holly's face was glowing with anticipation. She loved the tunnels; loved the industrious movement and purr of the machinery, the warm, humid atmosphere inside each tube, the thrill as the developing plants stretched up on their wires like sinuous acrobats and sprouted small shoots and leaves, then performed the astonishing and miraculous trick that was the production of a flower. Most of all she never failed to be excited by the appearance of the fruits and vegetables themselves, the stars, the leading roles in this theatrical show within each and every polytunnel.

Arriving at the porch-like structure which served as an entrance to Tunnel sixty, halfway along the row, Holly followed Laura as they waded through the scrub bath, where a sprinkler issued a gentle spray of bio-cleanser over their suits before they went in. The addition of filter shades completed their preparations, the overall look of alien visitors a fitting attire for the unearthly environment they were about to enter.

Tunnel sixty housed pepper and tomato plants. Since their requirements for growth were similar it made sense that they shared the same atmosphere. The enormous, arched tunnel was illuminated with intense, bright, light-solar simulation, necessitating the wearing of filter shades to avoid eye damage. In here the vigorous booming of the wind and steady pounding of rain on the plastic roof was barely audible due to a rigorous layer of sound insulation.

There was a low hum from the various machines;

the generator, the artificial pollinator, the sprinkler and heating systems. The atmosphere, redolent of a tropical paradise, was warm and damp, monitored and controlled by computer. Without the need of soil, nutrients were administered via an injection method into the water. These were pampered plants, whose every need was addressed, from hunger and thirst to warmth and freedom from disease; from fertilisation to production.

"Where are Dad and Farlow?"

Holly peered down the centre into the distance, between the regimented rows of climbing vines. At one kilometre long, it was impossible, even under the white light, to spot someone working at the opposite end of a tunnel. Her mother was consulting her wrist console.

"Farlow should be in here somewhere, down the other end with the tomatoes, perhaps. PAM says your father has gone next door to Greenergy to inspect some damage to the surveillance and the fencing. There was another break in last night."

Holly's stomach lurched.

"It's not far from us, is it? Would they try and break in here, to our tunnels, too?"

Laura shook her head, smiling at the child, although there had been incidences of food theft from production enterprises in some areas, a crime that was increasing at the same rate as the price of groceries.

"They don't seem interested in fruit and vegetables, love. It's always fuel they're after. And anyway, we'd know soon enough because the surveillance would spot them, the alarms would go off and PAM would tell us.

"Look! Farlow's on his way up here now."

A speck far down the central pathway was growing larger, becoming apparent as a bio-buggy ridden by a figure dressed as they were. It drew to a halt. Farlow dismounted, nodded to Laura and turned to Holly with his wide-eyed, engaging grin.

"Hello, Prof! Come to help out today? Your dad's been telling me all about your science centre tour yesterday. Reckon you'll be teaching us what we should be doing soon!"

Under her suit and shades, Holly felt her face go hot as it reddened to a crimson as deep as the tomatoes would be expected to acquire. The deep affection she held for Ewa, his wife, in no way obliterated the enduring crush she had on Farlow, her father's deputy. It was perpetuated by prolonged periods away from children her age, by his proximity and frequency of contact and by the way his light brown hair flopped over his blue eyes as he teased her with his wide, grinning mouth. That her daughter was under the spell of their co-worker had not escaped Laura but she'd accepted the situation as part of Holly's entry into adolescence, knowing that the young man would be no more likely to take advantage of her than retire to the Margins.

"I'm going to the control centre to check the levels and look over the STATS," she told Farlow. "Holly is going to stay and help with pollination today, is that OK

32

with you?"

"Great! I'll be glad of the extra pair of hands."

"Oh, and we'd like to come over and see how Ewa is doing, later. PAM's already messaged her so she knows we're going."

He laughed, winking at Holly and adding to her discomfort.

"I should think she's clinging to the expectation of your dropping in like a drowning woman! V-meet is no substitute for a visit in the flesh! She'll be able to bore you with all the latest stuff she's bought from up-cycle sites. We're running out of space in the new nursery, we have so many tiny outfits. This baby will be the best dressed tot in the hemisphere!"

A few minutes later, Holly was absorbed as she sat up in front of the controls that worked the pollen duster, moving with concentration up and down the rows to ensure application into each flower.

Joshua returned in time to join them for lunch, taken in the common room that served as Laura's office, reception area for inspectors, meeting room and dining space.

"Berenson's thinking of taking on extra security. This is the fourth burglary in six weeks, although they've only been successful twice. Still, they've managed to get about twenty barrels."

Holly was listening with rapt attention. She turned to Laura, eyes fearful, panic thumping through her.

"Holly, pop out and see if you can see Farlow

anywhere, would you? His lunch was ready ten minutes ago."

"PAM can ask him, Mum."

"Just have a look, please."

Holly breathed an exaggerated sigh before getting up, eliciting an amused smile from her father at the vestige of adolescent rebellion beginning to creep into her manner. She slid the door to behind her and stood still, heart thudding, to listen as her mother's voice lowered to an interesting conspiratorial level.

"She's nervous about the break in. I've reassured her they're not interested in stealing from our tunnels. I thought we should get our story straight. I don't want her having sleepless nights."

He frowned. "All right, but we will need to discuss our own security provision. Berenson's wondering about dogs."

"Dogs!"

Holly's eyes widened as a small gasp escaped her. Were they to have dogs on the farm? She might be able to help care for them; even to help train them.

"Yes. I know working dogs went out years ago, but apparently, they've started using them again in Scotland, where food and fuel theft is becoming a real issue. They can't prevent breaches altogether but they could buy enough time for us to get up here between PAM's alarm and they're getting away. They are bred and trained specifically, though, and come with a handler."

"Holly would be thrilled to have animals here. She's always poring over Dad's photos of the farm as it once was."

"Let's not pretend they'd be pets, love. These are not the fluffy farm animals from the old books on Hugh's shelves. They are trained, animal assault machines. They would live in separate area, outside, probably within a cordoned off passage between the outside perimeter fence and the tunnels. They would be more dangerous to us than any burglar, so we'd need to be especially careful around them, or anywhere near them."

Holly re-entered the small office and flung herself on to a rudimentary bench made from pallets, inserting a nonchalance into her tone and staring at the floor.

"Farlow will be a few minutes. He's just finishing cleaning the spray heads."

Her cheeks were still hot from the exchange with the young man. Laura glanced down at her wrist console.

"Three-hour forecast, please PAM."

"A dry break is coming over in thirty-six minutes," PAM intoned. "The break will last for two hours twenty minutes. Showers will follow."

Two hours! There would be time to do some outside repairs. Joshua stood up abruptly.

"I'll get along and have a look along this section. Farlow can meet me when he's had lunch. I'll let him know where I've got to. I'll see you later." He planted a brisk kiss on the cheeks of both before leaving.

"Twenty-four-hour forecast, please PAM." Laura moved back to her swivel seat by the big screen and switched on the visuals.

"Dry break in thirty-three minutes; two hours twenty. Showers for three hours fifty minutes. Increasing wind. Clear break for eight hours thirty minutes, followed by steady rain."

Laura stared at the screen then around at her daughter, who'd come to stand behind her chair. She called up Josh.

"Had the forecast?"

"Yes. We have two hours, don't we?"

"Yes, but the wind is going to get up. It'll blow a clear patch over tonight. We should try to get outside. I'll ask PAM to message Hugh so that he can prepare the telescope."

Holly was grinning and fidgeting with anticipation. "Can I stay up? I can't remember the last time I saw the moon! Can I?"

Laura stood up and hugged her. "Tell you what. Get to bed at a sensible time and we'll wake you when we're ready to go out. I don't want you losing your beauty sleep, especially as you're off on a tour tomorrow! Come on, now; we should get over to see Ewa or the day will be over."

Holly

Since almost all the journey to Farlow and Ewa's cottage could be completed via a tunnel, Laura and Holly opted to walk rather than take the buggy and, besides, Josh and Farlow needed both vehicles to complete maintenance tasks and check around the perimeter of each tube. Strolling down the central pathway, Laura paused here and there to examine foliage or flowers, looking closely at a stem, the stamens inside some petals or the underside of a leaf. Despite their stringent hygiene measures and their rigid adherence to anti disease guidelines at Earthsend Farm they could never afford to relax, as the possibility of pests or fungal infection was never off their minds.

On the outside, wild plants fared less well despite the past efforts of countless biologists and environmental groups to preserve them. Resources for such projects had dwindled with the growing necessity for them to be directed at food production. Land, research and man hours must be focused on feeding and housing the world's population rather than trying to preserve wild species. As they walked, Laura told Holly she felt wistful when she saw how many trees and wild flowers were no longer a feature of the landscape, and uneasy about the loss. Surely the purpose of so much diversity was more than decoration? Would the careless shedding of wild trees, plants, mammals and insects play some part in a future catastrophe, just as cavalier use of the planet's natural resources in the past had produced today's problems?

Emerging from the tunnel end they threw off the waterproof hoods of their suits, both faces upturned to the sky, which had lightened. There was movement in the cloud now as a breeze picked up, hurrying the billowing tracts along like pale, rushing ghosts. A quiet, dry interval, even of two hours, could induce celebratory feelings and it was in a euphoric mood that they arrived at the cottage door where Ewa was standing, waiting to receive them.

If it were possible, Holly thought Ewa James was even more beautiful in late pregnancy than she'd been before; a pink glow lit up her skin, her body had become full and rounded like a luscious, ripe peach, her face bore a calm, fulfilled expression with a half-smile as if to protect a precious secret. After they'd shed their cumbersome suits, she hugged them both before leading them into the tiny kitchen, where the evidence of recent baking was laid out.

"It's all ready. Shall we take tea outside? We should not waste the dry time, I think."

There was little left of Ewa's Polish accent now, except for a slight, unnatural formality of speech that simply added to her charm. Her attributes of good communication, empathy and insight had made her the ideal choice when Joshua looked amongst his small workforce for a liaison officer, so when Farlow, his right-hand man, fell headlong in love with her it had seemed to complete the entire outfit, as if a final piece of jigsaw had been inserted to portray the whole picture. Living as they did on the farm estate, they were considered part of the extended family, and soon to be augmented by a small newcomer, a baby boy due in less than a month; an event that Holly anticipated with a mixture of awe and feverish excitement.

"You look well, Ewa," Laura said when they were seated outside with tea and cake. "I assume all your v-med checks have gone well?"

Ewa leaned back against the cottage's stone wall, stroking the swollen mound of her belly. Holly watched, fascinated by the distended shape of her, by her languorous, blousy countenance and dreamy speech. She hung, almost breathless on Ewa's every word, wanting to know everything, every detail about the developing baby and the birth plan.

"Oh yes, of course he is growing very well. He is a good weight already. Farlow will take me to Longhope village, to the med-pod on the tenth of next month. That is just three days before the due date. We should be able to come home after one week, I think."

Ewa was accustomed to the fact, thinking nothing of having to be sterilised in the immediate aftermath of her baby's birth. She had never known anything different, and neither would Holly.

The single child policy had been in place for ten years now; one of the first pieces of legislation brought in since European government had moved to Basel, and one that most of the rest of the world had been quick to follow as the increase in the global population became critical.

"So, Holly, Farlow has been telling me you are going to Dry-camp in a few days. What activities will you do this time? Will you do some sport?"

She turned her blue eyes on to Holly, who became bashful under her gaze, but was excited all the same, anticipating the four days she would spend in the company of her fellow pupils, undertaking team building and social skills exercises in the community pod at Longhope village.

"I've chosen handball, climbing and soccer for my sports this time. We'll have a production to do so I'll be taking part in the choir and we have to show our history presentations for the teachers and the other students to grade."

"It sounds like fun and hard work. What is your history presentation about?"

"We had to find out as much as we could about our home; when it was built, who has lived there and how it has changed."

"What about the kids who have moved from flood zones? It will be hard for them, I think. If you have to be rehomed into new buildings there will not be so much history to discover."

Holly nodded. "Mrs Philips said they can choose to find out about where they came from or the new place they've moved to."

They were all silent for a few minutes, thinking about the latest group of families who'd had to relocate to higher ground and be rehoused, most in apartments in ecologically sound, high-rise buildings, leaving behind them loved homes with gardens they'd made their own; now ruined, useless and underwater. Luckier, wealthier families had been able to move into the newer pontoon estates that had sprung up this century, where the homes would rise and fall with the water. But we are the luckiest of all, Holly thought; those of us whose homes and livelihoods can stay where we always were, on the high ground to begin with.

Though the girl had tried to stay alert she'd succumbed to sleep and had to be woken by her mother in the eerie half-light that permeated through the eco-blinds; moonlight. She fumbled in her eagerness to dress, instructed by Laura to don warm clothing, as the dry break brought with it a sharp, unaccustomed burst of cold. Her father and grandfather were already out in the garden, setting up the telescope to find the best angle and adjusting binoculars, having extinguished the house lights to provide the dark backdrop necessary for viewing.

She tilted her head up to stare at the sky. It was magical, an inky canvas painted with sparkling pinpricks of stars, like a chorus of ballerinas supporting the principal dancer, the plump, enigmatic, silver moon. She joined Hugh at the telescope to look through and marvel at the intricate landscape on its surface, listening while he described the volcanoes, craters and fissures and the discoveries that were made nearly two hundred years ago when men had travelled there and even set foot upon its dark, dusty ground; astronauts taking huge, floating steps in its weight-reducing atmosphere and wearing bulky suits to enable breathing. The stories were enthralling. Manned space exploration had ceased almost a hundred years ago, when it was deemed a drain on the earth's resources for no useful return.

As she gazed at the silver disc hanging serene and ethereal above, she made out the ghostly face of ancient rhyme:

"The man in the moon came tumbling down
And asked his way to Norwich.
He went by the south and burnt his mouth
With supping cold pease porridge."

"Granddad, where is Norwich?"

"Where *was* Norwich? It was a real place, Holly, a city in the east of England, an area they called East Anglia. It was mostly flat, agricultural land, with wonderful, fertile soil; a major area for cultivation, producing much of what people ate, all underwater now of course like many places, including a whole country called the Netherlands."

Joshua pointed to the three stars of Orion's belt.

"Do you remember the last time we looked? See if you can pick some of the constellations out for yourself this time."

Although Holly felt she wanted to stay out under the stars for ever, it was cold and she was persuaded in with the promise of hot chocolate. The dry spell was due to continue into the next day so Hugh arranged with Laura to have a few hours outside. He'd work in the garden vegetable beds and perhaps go out with the gun to bag some wild rabbits. It would be a welcome treat for them all to eat real, fresh meat.

Holly

Every twelve weeks Mrs Philips and her staff met with her class of children to share activities in a large eco-pod with a retractable domed roof, part of a community complex that served a large administrative area surrounding Longhope village. The community pod consisted of education, health, sport, recreation and local government units as well as grocery and up-cycling outlets.

The education unit was equipped with a canteen and small dormitories and showers to accommodate the children during their stay. Divided into work parties, they would be sourcing and preparing their own meals as well as undertaking a variety of activities designed to address their physical and social skills and general development. Dry-camp also gave Mrs Philips an opportunity to relate to her pupils in reality and ascertain their emotional development, an aspect in which v-checks were still not as adept as human professionals.

Children were drawn from both the immediate and the outlying administrative area, taking part on a rotation basis, class by class. For the majority, the four days every three months were an interval to be anticipated with great pleasure, when every meticulously planned moment was packed with learning potential, an extensive range of activities on offer; art, music, theatre, sport, communication, play, technology, team building-skills and knowledge that still needed to be delivered by humans to groups of humans rather than by computer to individuals.

For Holly the most significant feature of Dry-camp was meeting up with her friends, a situation that, to her mind, could not be simulated by v-meeting, no matter how realistic 3D imagery and holograms became. Familiar with the routine, she hoisted her pack up on to her customary bunk before going to assemble in the main dome with Mrs Philips. As she paused for a moment to message a few words of reassurance to her mother on her wrist console she felt a pair of skinny, brown arms encircle her waist and squeeze tight. Nell!

"What time did you get here?" Holly hugged her best friend.

"Only about two minutes before you! Let's hurry up and get to assembly so we can be in the same chef group. Did you finish your presentation? I can't wait for choir, can you?"

Holly laughed as Nell erupted into her usual enthusiastic outburst. A small, wiry, vivacious girl, she liked to throw herself into as many activities as she could fit into the schedule, encouraged by her wealthy parents who were protective of her future. They worked in marine and dockside commerce, living in one of the better parts of the pontoon estate, a privileged oasis. Holly had glimpsed her friend's luxurious surroundings during their frequent v-meets, but while she was impressed, she knew she'd never want to swap her tiny bedroom in the eaves of the farmhouse for Nell's designer custom-build. The girls ran off together to the main dome to begin the day's activities.

Later, after supper, the children and staff reassembled in the dome for the first of the history presentations, assignments that had been undertaken by distance learning and were now to be graded. They were multi-media projects, each lasting about three minutes. Holly and Nell paid close attention to the first few, gauging the standard against their own creations; then it was Holly's turn. She stood to introduce it before pressing the key to start the film. Her narration began as the camera panned in to a close up of their farmhouse:

"Earthsend Farm has been in my family for generations. It is said that the first farmers came to the hillside and thought there could never be anywhere more beautiful even if they travelled to the ends of the earth, so they named it 'Earthsend'. Long ago, when my grandfather, Hugh, was a boy, animals were farmed here for meat and other products. There were sheep and hens.

Holly had toured the farm, filming the interiors of the old stone barns where the livestock had been housed.

"These are the feed troughs and the drinking

troughs the animals used. There are still remains of some of the old baths that were used outside in the fields for animals to drink from. In those days people didn't realise that it was not a good use of land to raise animals to be killed and eaten.

"Nowadays my father, Joshua, and mother, Laura, use the land area to produce vegetables and fruit..."

She looked around at her audience, reassured by their attentive gaze, and continued.

Ethan

Futura was a sturdy, resilient vessel. She could withstand the most torrential downfalls and run before the strongest gales. She was watertight, buoyant and strong. Her freight capacity was large for such a compact, manoeuvrable craft and she was versatile enough to travel the rivers, canals and the open sea with ease. She was as easy to handle under sail as with the use of her solar and bio-fuel engine.

In many ways, Futura resembled an ancient schooner, like those that sailed in the nineteenth century, but sailors of yesteryear would not have recognised the materials that made up her hull, the technologies that ran her systems, her complicated power sources or her sophisticated security structure.

Today she was making steady progress along the channel towards Dusseldorf, achieving a good time in the choppy seas and relentless, grey rain, her light, indestructible sails hauling her along despite a hold full of Greenergy's bio-fuel. Ethan Conway leant on the forward rail, perusing the undulating waves, standing as firm and solid as a stone while a barrage of salty, white-topped rollers buffeted the sides.

Two years of living and working on board had

endowed Ethan with the ability to cope with Futura single-handed, but he needed Hooper, now, to teach him the business of trading; the ability to build a network of contacts, liaise with port authorities, foster new links and sever less profitable ones; the skills to manage a crew of his own and to defend the ship against occasional gangs of marauding pirates.

At first Hooper had been sceptical, reluctant to take on a seventeen-year-old 'landlubber' as she called the boy, unconvinced that the lad could be committed until Joshua had persuaded her with a generous subsidy towards Ethan's apprenticeship. She'd looked the boy up and down, noticing his slender, gangly limbs and slight frame and doubted he'd have the strength or the stamina for long days at sea, where even modern machinery and mechanisms were not able to deal with every chore, or cope with any emergency.

Now her head and shoulders appeared from the companionway, wind ruffling the short cropped, black mop of hair.

"Ethan, chow is ready in the galley if you want. We can leave her on automatic for a while."

Ethan climbed down into the small living area. He'd become accustomed now to sharing the tiny space, with its cramped galley and living and dining area like a doll's house and his capsule of a bunk in part of a passage. He'd even got used to living with the blunt, enigmatic woman who was his boss, mentor and only companion during their voyages, earning her respect after many long days at sea when he'd finally managed to prove himself in her eyes. But despite the number of hours they'd spent in each other's company she'd never revealed anything about herself or her past; how she had acquired her mariner skills or the funds to acquire Futura and all her equipment. At thirty-four, Hooper was almost twice his age and whilst a beautiful, striking mix of Chinese and European parents her reaction to everyone she met was confined to brisk, business-like efficiency.

She studied the screen while they ate.

"Making good time. At this rate we'll be in on schedule. The only thing is, there seems to be some kind of alert. I'm getting a message to v-meet the harbour manager at Dusseldorf. The weather is OK. We should be there in about five hours. I'll speak to him in a minute, when we've eaten. What do you think he wants?"

Ethan studied the view from the small cabin window, where the undulating waves rose and fell like iron grey horses on a fairground carousel. He swallowed a mouthful of sandwich.

"Pirates? They could be between us and the port?"

She frowned at the screen, the almond pools of her eyes narrowing.

"PAM would have alerted us to pirates by now if that were the case."

He thought.

"They may have blocked it, or hacked into the

system. What if they're holding him hostage?"

Hooper treated him to one of her withering expressions, honed during the two years he'd been in her tutelage.

"If they'd blocked the transmission, we wouldn't have received the message. And I don't see how they'd get through the port security. It's all much too tight these days for them to breach it. That's why they only attack in the open sea. They would also know what we're carrying and it would hardly be worth the risk for the size of cargo. It might be different if we had passengers. No, it must be something else."

Ethan experienced a small frisson of unease, more from the perplexity of his boss's expression than from the puzzling message. His apprenticeship aboard Futura had so far been unmarred by any events more challenging than severe storms or smugglers and to see Hooper, whose competence he equated with that of Sir Francis Drake, the historic figure of Elizabethan times, nonplussed, was in itself a disquieting experience.

She turned back to the screen.

"PAM, get me Captain Engel."

After a few seconds the harbour manager's face appeared on screen.

"Ms Hooper, thank you for your prompt response."

The middle-aged man looked drawn and grey, the appearance of one who has slept little and had a heavy burden of worry to bear. He was seated in a cramped office, his elbows resting on a desk.

"What can we do for you, Captain?"

"I have to ask you not to dock. The port is closed. I am aware that you are carrying a cargo and that it is a valuable consignment of fuel, but the port here at Dusseldorf is in lockdown. We are unable, at present, to allow any vessel in or out."

As Hooper swung around to Ethan, her face bore the frowning glint of annoyance with which he was familiar. She made the loud clucking sound that he knew signified severe irritation and he was relieved for once, not to be on the receiving end of her displeasure.

"We are on schedule to deliver our cargo, Captain. What do you suggest we do?"

"Your options are to sail north-east to Hanover or Berlin and unload. There is no problem in either port at present; or you can turn back, or you could drop anchor out in the bay here, where there is still shelter and wait it out, provided that no one disembarks or attempts to come into port."

"May I ask what the problem is?"

He raised his eyes to hers. They were two, red rimmed slits.

"It's a quarantine order. We are locked down for a virus. No one comes in or out, that's the order."

"How long?"

He shrugged. "Two or three weeks, perhaps. I need to know your decision. If you choose to stay out in the harbour, I will have to make other shipping aware of your position and so on. Your decision may depend on your supplies, of course, how many days' water and food you have."

"We are still some hours out. We'll check our supplies and talk to our buyer then let you know as soon as possible."

The screen darkened. Ethan swung down through the small hatchway to look at the water tanks and see how their food supply was going before returning to the cabin. They were good for two weeks, three if they were careful. Hooper had a representative from the company that was buying the fuel on screen, a fish farm near Krefeld, a little down the coast. The fish farmer knew of the emergency and was resigned to waiting, with no means of collecting the barrels from further north.

"At least they are prepared to wait."

Ethan sought to make the best of their dilemma, but his boss pouted, not so easily soothed.

"Time is money, Ethan. Don't forget we also have to load machine parts for Re-New and deliver them by next Friday. The parts will be there, somewhere by the pontoons, waiting to be loaded. I'd better message them next. While we are stuck here with nothing to do, we aren't making any money."

He went up on deck, telling her he'd check the rigging was secure, although it was more a need to escape her paranoia than anything. On the horizon the land mass was appearing, pale against the grey sea, and with less than an hour to port he could make out the dark shapes of assorted vessels standing out to sea in the opening to the Wesel Channel, their bare masts reaching up into a troubled, oppressive sky. He leaned against Futura's rail, looking down as she cut an efficient furrow through the choppy waves. They would be a sitting target in the outer harbour, where an assembly of cargo and passenger ships was gathering, he thought. Pirate gangs or worse still, terrorists and extortionists, would know by now of the quarantine order; would know that there were fat profits to be made if they moved in now. Then a worse and much more frightening idea came to him. Supposing a gang was using bio-terrorism to isolate the port? They may have insinuated a virus into the community, either with a human 'mule' or by contamination. It would not be the first time such a situation had arisen. However quick the authorities were to act the security forces on the pontoon-side would be compromised as personnel fell prey to the virus. It was a disturbing possibility, and one that he would put to his boss.

No one knew where or how much virus serum was stored in illicit laboratories around the world. As long as a single phial of influenza, rabies or Ebola existed anywhere it would have the capability of being manufactured into amounts great enough to threaten communities and cause entire populations to be wiped out. Scientists everywhere were continuing to try and find an alternative to the antibiotics that were widely used a hundred years ago to control disease but, so far, the only effective means of minimising the effects was prevention, hence the quarantine procedure at Dusseldorf. Ethan wondered what the disease was. He would try to find out once Hooper was finished with all her negotiations. If it was something like influenza there would be a limited number of casualties amongst the very old and the very young but the main body of the community would recover after a few weeks. If it were a more sinister disease such as rabies there would be carnage.

As one of the smaller vessels, Futura was allocated a slot further in than most and nearer to the pontoons and unloading bays. This meant that Ethan could sail her in up the Wesel Channel without the use of the bio-engine until the final manoeuvre. He counted twenty-three units of shipping as they progressed towards their berth on water that was quieter now that they were in the lee of the channel.

When they dropped anchor, he could see they were placed between a cargo ketch much like Futura and what appeared to be a private leisure or living craft, neither of which was any larger than their own boat. There was no one on the deck of either. From this vantage point, while it was possible to see the pontoons with the naked eye, Ethan decided to go down for the binoculars in order to ascertain how much activity there was on the dockside. Hooper was engaged in a heated argument with her contact at Re-New, the recycling depot that was expecting their delivery of machine parts to Guildford, where it seemed that Futura's crew would be held personally accountable for a failure to meet targets and that remuneration would be adjusted as a consequence. When the conversation finished without resolution, he realised it was not the best time to raise his concerns about the virus, nevertheless Ethan drew in a breath and told her.

Hooper stared out of the porthole while he spoke then swivelled back to the screen.

"OK, we'll take a look at the pontoons. They may give us a clue."

Futura's system locked into the security camera footage of the floating dockside. There were no vessels docked close in, or evidence of any commercial activity. The camera panned around the area, entirely still and silent, like an abandoned, underwater city. There were plenty of those on the planet these days. Ethan peered over the woman's shoulder.

"There!" he cried, pointing.

A figure swathed in a bio-suit sauntered along in front of one of the giant, floating warehouses. The figure was carrying a weapon.

"Port security," Hooper shrugged.

"How do you know? The bio-suits don't make it clear, do they? Another thing I don't understand is there are no drones overhead. What's happened to them? We can't get an aerial view without them."

He was right. In normal circumstances there would be unmanned Heli craft beaming surveillance down to security. She sighed, irritated.

"All right. Just to set your mind at rest. I'll get Engel back again. PAM, can you get Captain Engel?"

There was momentary fuzz on the screen before it blacked out. At last Hooper looked concerned. A vast amount of shipping had amassed in the channel and might now be captive. Ethan consulted his wrist console which responded as he expected; no signal. All means of communication had been obliterated.

Startled by the sound of a voice from somewhere outside they both darted up on to the deck. Two crew members on the ketch were calling across the short stretch of water to them. Ethan waved back.

"Hello, do you know what's going on? We've no signal."

The older of the two men leaned on the ketch's rail in the fading twilight. Ethan noted that the ship, Caravel, was registered to Portugal.

"No, no signal. Something not right."

"Listen!" Hooper cocked her head at the sound of a distant motor. She looked at Ethan then called to the two sailors.

"Better get below. Check your security. Let's go!"

They fled down the stairs and looked out into the darkening night. The sea lapped against Futura's sides, oily under the vessel's lights as the motor noise grew louder, buzzing like an angry wasp. The motor boat drew closer until Ethan could make out three or four figures, bulky in their suits. They seemed to be laying out a net of some kind from the rear of the boat as they went. Surely not fishing?

Hooper murmured, "They're laying a net. I don't like it!"

The boat continued past them and on down the channel, continuing to lay down a netting barrier as it went. In its wake, floats indicated the path of the web, trapping all the shipping that had anchored there.

"It's just a net. What's to stop us cutting through?"

They were soon to find out. A second motor dinghy approached from the pontoons, slowing as it came level with Futura and Caravel. An amplified voice boomed out across the water, echoing eerily in the cold atmosphere.

"Fellow seamen and women, please stay calm and no harm will come to anyone. We must warn you to stay at berth. Do not attempt to draw anchor and leave. We have put down a mined net which will explode on contact with any object. We will shortly be approaching each of you to relieve you of your cargos. We have full details of the contents of your holds, so please do not attempt to conceal anything. When your cargo has been discharged you will be released and free to leave. I repeat, do not try to resist or get underway."

The voice was cultured, business-like, with an underlying, clipped quality indicating that an accent had been suppressed. The small boat moved further along towards the larger ships, where it paused again to deliver its message. Ethan turned to his boss.

"We have to get out."

She shook her head.

"You heard what they said. We can't pass over a mine net! We'd be blown to blazes."

He began to tear off his outer clothing.

"I'm going down. I'll take the wire cutters. I'm going to cut us an outlet through the net. We can ditch the barrels as we go — it'll make us faster and maybe we'll be able to salvage the cargo at a later date. See if you can get back to Caravel. They might want to follow us through and there'd be safety in numbers."

Hooper's eyes blazed.

"You can't do that! It'll be suicide, Ethan. Better to let them have the cargo. The insurance will have to cover it."

He was pulling on diving gear.

"You don't think they're telling the truth, do you? They have no intention of freeing us. Look at what they've done to the port! They are ruthless. If they are happy to contaminate the population of Dusseldorf, knowing that many will not survive whatever disease they've planted, they aren't going to let us sail away into the horizon, are they? They'll want our craft, at least. Do you want some outlaw to have Futura?"

Now he saw the panic in her face. This was where it hit home.

"Let me do it, then. Futura is my baby. It's down to me to save her."

He zipped up, shrugged on the lightweight tank vest and pulled a mask down around his neck.

"That's just why you need to be the one to steer her through the gap. Anyway, I'm ready now and I don't think we can waste time. You go up and get Caravel's attention. I'm going to slip into the water at the stern while they're further up the channel. When I think I'm through the net I'll tap twice on the hull with the wire cutters. You will need to be ready with the engine running. With luck they won't be back yet, or they won't hear our engine above their own. Drop a line over the side and I'll catch hold. When we're well clear you can haul me back in."

He pulled on a head flashlight and made towards the stairs. She put a hand on his arm.

"Ethan…"

He paused. She never uttered his name, only ever issued instructions or barked reprimands.

"Let's go," he said. "We have no time."

He leapt up and out, barefoot, on to the deck. Across the water he caught sight of the two Portuguese, back on the deck of Caravel and gestured at them with the cutters before shinning over the rail, hanging for a moment then slipping, with little more than a ripple into the unctuous water. She watched his progress along the side then lost him as he dived deeper.

As yet there was no sign of a returning boat.

"We're making a break," she hissed to Caravel's crewmen. "Follow as close as you can when I give the signal."

The taller Portuguese waved an automatic rifle.

"We give you cover," he replied, nodding.

Hooper descended the stairs and went to the dashboard where she pressed the button to start the engine. It purred into action and she offered silent, automatic thanks to an unnamed deity for the instant response and for the smooth, efficient quietness of the vessel's idling mode. She turned down the revs as far as she could to further suppress the sound and waited, peering out at the water and listening for the whine of the pirates' boats. After a few minutes she darted up on deck for a furtive scan of the channel then caught the distant buzz of engines. They must have turned back. She bit her lip, breathing fast and feeling the sweat trickle down her neck.

Across the gap the Portuguese sailor, rifle poised, was staring out in the same direction towards the open sea in an attempt to spot the returning boats. They glanced at each other. Hooper gestured, revolving her hands to signal an enquiry, 'should they lift the anchors?' He shrugged then nodded, turning to call down to his colleague. The woman ran back down to the controls and set the anchor in motion, straining to hear the clanging tap that would herald Ethan's return. The seconds ticked painfully on as the sound of the pirates' engines grew louder. From the window she saw a glow on the sea as the shafts of their lights approached. Within another few seconds she could hear their shouts.

"Ethan," she whispered. "Please hurry!"

Then she heard it — weak but unmistakeable; the

muffled clang of something hitting the hull underwater. She held her nerve for another five seconds before moving Futura forward as fast as she dare, although a quick glance out of the port window told her the smaller craft would be upon her almost immediately, and she gunned the engine, trusting that Ethan would have gained the safety of the line by now.

There were startled cries from the water then a rushing sound followed by a splash, before the explosion blasted her ears, rocking Futura so that she bucked, throwing Hooper to her knees. Would Ethan be able to hold on? She had to hope so. She pressed on regardless of the ensuing downpour of rockets that were pelting down in a deadly storm, causing the vessel to buck and toss in the maelstrom. From somewhere to stern she heard gunfire mingled with the shouts and continuing barrage as Caravel's crew retaliated, attempting to pick off the attacking pirates. She chanced a quick look over her shoulder and saw a bigger flash that could only have emanated from one of the larger vessels. With no hope of attaining their own freedom they must be offering some additional support.

In the illuminated shaft of Futura's lights she saw the second speedboat circle around in an arc and disappear to stern, presumably in a bid to isolate both the yacht and Caravel but she could do nothing; nothing except to keep on and hope they would give up the chase. After all they were only two small transport yachts with limited spoils.

There was an urgent need to check on Ethan. She set some coordinates and left Futura on automatic before making her way to the stairway, holding on as the floor slid this way and that under the continual bursts of rocket fire. She hauled herself up the steps as repeated impacts shook the boat's hull. Strengthened with Graphene, the outer casing seemed, so far, to be resisting the attack but it was impossible to gauge what weaponry they were using.

Needing to stay low, she crawled out on to the deck, which was awash as a continual, foaming assault of seawater rose up to engulf it; back and forth as the deck floor tipped at alarming angles. She grasped a line and hooked it to her harness then gained the stern rail, searching for the rope she'd dropped, gasping as each new wall of water fell over her. The line was still there where she'd secured it. She grabbed it and hauled, one handed, expecting the weight of resistance, bracing her body against the tilting side in preparation for the pull as she withdrew the rope, screaming over the flash and roar of gunfire and rocket explosions.

But the line held nothing. There was no resistance as she pulled it in, staring aghast as the naked end of the rope appeared. Ethan was not there.

Joshua

Josh turned the engine off. There was no point in wasting valuable fuel. From their place in the queue on the Pontoon Road he and Farlow watched the gathering crowd of protesters as they milled about by the waterside brandishing banners and chanting, hoods up against the relentless, blustery rain.

"What are they saying this time?"

Farlow lifted the magnifiers to peer out of the side window through the small rivulets forming on the glass.

"It's the usual issues, I think — food prices, fuel prices, flooding, homelessness. I suppose the coming election will have stirred up more unrest. A lot of people who wouldn't have been interested in politics twenty years ago realise what's at stake now, so they can't afford to be apathetic."

On the periphery of the crowd there was a modest but significant police presence. Farlow continued to scan the quayside, panning round with the magnifiers.

"Josh, what's going to happen if Power Alliance gets a majority this time?"

Joshua rubbed his eyes. He felt stretched from lack of sleep. He shook his head.

"We can't know what they'll do, but it won't be

good for us, that's for sure. Berenson's hinting about takeovers; starting to get impatient now that I've made it clear I'm not interested in selling up. He may know more than he lets on. Once Power Alliance gets into government there'll be nothing to prevent a monopoly of all the industries. Food, recycling, water, transport, construction, even media will belong to them."

"How can they do that? How can they take businesses and livelihoods from people?"

"It isn't without precedent, Far. Throughout history there were revolutions and dictatorships all over the world. In Russia, back in the twentieth century the regime was overthrown and the owned lands were redistributed.

"Thing is, the way the fuel prices are going we will have to think seriously about how we can continue to run independently anyway. It would be different if there was another provider, but there isn't. Greenergy have bio-fuel all sown up. Berenson knows that when the price of running the tunnels becomes too much, we'll have no option."

The younger man lowered the magnifiers as a gust of wind rocked the vehicle and splattered the windscreen with a squally burst of rain.

"Suppose that happens. What will we do?"

Joshua placed a large, calloused hand on his companion's shoulder, recognising the fear in him, a man with responsibilities now; a wife and a small baby to care for.

"Oh, I don't doubt they'll keep us on as managers. We are very good at our job so it wouldn't be worth replacing us. But they would probably put a lot more security in and tighten up regulations, inspections and so on. We wouldn't be working for ourselves any longer."

PAM buzzed from the dashboard console.

"Josh, it's Laura for you."

"Josh? Darling, we've had some news! Hooper thinks he may be ready to come out in a week or so. He'll be able to come to us until the transplant is ready!"

"God! I can't believe it! That is wonderful."

He closed his eyes and breathed out, wanting to be at home with her, wanting to share the relief together.

"I was hoping to be finished here and back this afternoon but we are caught up in a protest. It is blocking the Pontoon Road. It looks as if the police are going to clear a way through. I'll keep you up to date."

"Yes, I can see it on screen. Take care though because we've a severe weather front coming over. Your window for unloading is quite narrow; less than an hour until it freshens into cyclone conditions. You'll need to get back, too."

The men exchanged looks.

"At least," suggested Farlow, "the worsening weather will disperse the crowd."

Twenty minutes later they reached the unloading bay and leapt out into the now turbulent wind and angry rain that precluded the coming cyclone. Zipped and hooded they raced to unburden the truck, working together to place the large cartons of vegetables on to a trolley and manoeuvring it into the shelter of the bay then placing each box into a tidy stack ready for collection by the next water transport.

By the time they'd finished, the entire dock area was wracked by the strengthening storm, the pontoons bucking and dipping like wild horses and choppy, white-edged waves leaping up to buffet the vessels at their moorings. As predicted, the crowd of protesters had melted away leaving a few bits of poster to spiral up in furious eddies and abandoned placards to slide before the wind.

They ran to tug open the truck's doors, faces streaming from the rain, which was beating down in sporadic squalls.

Josh's eyes blazed as he climbed in.

"Let's go. I want to know everything about Ethan!"

They were all in Hugh's living room, squeezed together on the sofas as Doctor Lena Akers explained Ethan's treatment and what to expect when he arrived for a convalescent period prior to receiving his transplant. The image was given to occasional flickering and freezing whenever a particularly strong gust of wind obliterated the signal, causing Laura to frown in frustrated irritation and Joshua to cast anxious glances at the window. Now and then random bits of vegetation flew past or battered the glass and a few slates seemed to have slipped off the roof and on to the path.

Since knowing of her brother's return to them, Holly had been in a turmoil of alternating excitement and trepidation, exasperating to her parents; thrilled at the notion of Ethan, who'd she'd not seen for over two years, coming back to live with them and anxious over the issue of his terrible injury. Joshua allowed himself a faint smile to see her holding her breath as she focused with rapt attention on the doctor's indistinct representation, hovering in the room like a ghost as she spoke.

"The arm we have given him at present is electronic. This will serve two purposes. It will prepare his nervous system for adaptation to the replacement and he will get a significant amount of use from the mechanical device while he has it. Of course, it will not be as competent as the new arm, but we have to wait for it to grow. Once it is completed and reattached, he should not notice any difference from the original."

Laura leaned forward towards the doctor's image.

"When can we see him?"

A slight smile creased the corner of Lena Aker's mouth as she fixed her gaze on Ethan's mother, assessing Laura's manner for calm resilience.

"It might be best at this stage for just one of you to meet with him, Mrs Conway." Joshua frowned, eager as his wife to see for himself the extent of their son's injuries.

"He has been through a trauma which has left him emotionally drained as well as the physical difficulties one expects with loss of limbs. I understand you have not physically met your son for some time; two years or so?"

Laura shook her head. "Ethan has been away at sea for almost all of that time. We've had regular v-meetings but he hasn't been home."

This was the way now. Unless, like Ethan, you travelled for work there was little opportunity for seeing the world. In the old days, when Hugh was a boy, almost everyone travelled for leisure purposes; to see foreign countries, to enjoy different climates or to undertake active pursuits. Laura had seen history footage of how people used to holiday in the days before fuel costs, world conflicts and climate crises had restricted foreign travel for pleasure to a luxury only the very wealthy could access; energy executives, mainly.

"I'll meet him in private, Doctor," she told Lena. "Just give me a minute. I can go to the study and reconnect."

She left the room as a violent gust of wind carrying a squall of rain hit the window in a sudden blast that drew the attention of the others. Joshua's fleeting disappointment at being excluded from this first sight of his son was soon eclipsed by anxiety. PAM's green light flashed in rapid urgency as the messenger kicked in.

"Josh, Farlow on screen."

The young man spoke quickly, his face stricken, stifling his burgeoning panic.

"Josh — I've been keeping an eye on the tunnels

since we got back from port. Sixty is in trouble. About half of the roof is off and at least half the stock is destroyed. There are two more tunnels where the fixings have come loose, the wind is getting up underneath and it won't be long before they go the same way. I'm going out to see if I can secure them before any more damage is done."

Joshua got to his feet, looking away from Farlow at the angry blasts and bent over trees outside, catching a glimpse of a substantial branch as it broke from the old apple tree and blew out of view, hearing the ominous slide of another slate as it was freed from its mooring on the roof to hurtle towards the gutter. He shook his head at the screen.

"Stay inside, man. You'd be mad to go out in this. We have to let it run its course."

"I can fix it, Josh. It won't take much. I only need to batten down the covers. I can save the two flapping tunnels, at least."

Joshua looked at Holly, deliberating.

"Tell your mother I'm going out to meet Farlow at the tunnels."

"I'm coming too, Dad! I can help!"

"NO! I need you to help here. Stay in, Holly. I want you to stay by the screen, please, and make sure everyone knows what's going on. I really need you to do this, OK?"

He took her by the shoulders, looking intently until she nodded then he strode out to the lobby.

Holly switched the screen on to tunnel surveillance, selecting Tunnel sixty, gasping as it came into view, a ruinous maelstrom of tattered plastic and mangled machinery; nothing left of the verdant jungle of plants or their fruit, the product of her labours earlier in the year. She switched to another camera and panned along the length of the installation. At least half the tunnels appeared to have parts of their roofs missing, or to have become loose from the fixings, the grey sheeting no longer rigid but flapping like sails. Their interiors would be prey to the elements; the more delicate plants would be destroyed. As she watched, tunnel components continued to break away and escape into the sky, tossed beyond view.

She panned around to the fencing, the tall, electric barrier between the installation and the security corridor where the dogs were kept. A blurred shape skittered past, then another, running in a frenzy, unhinged by the tumult. She homed in along the length of the fence and paused to pull back as she spotted something new, pulling back to inspect it. A long piece of tunnel frame was caught on the fence; had weighed it almost to the ground. The security corridor was breached. She caught her breath, knowing it could only be minutes before the dogs found the gap, knowing they were killers.

"PAM, get me Joshua please."

He responded instantly. "Yes Holly." He was shouting above the roaring wind.

"Dad, where are you?"

"I'm nearly at the security corridor gate. I can see…"

The next words were obliterated by the wind.

"Dad! The fence outside seventy-four is down!" The girl yelled at the screen, willing the words to be heard. "I've seen the dogs running. They can get through. Don't go in!"

She strained to hear his reply above the howling gale.

"Holly — message Farlow. I…"

His voice disappeared, cut off. PAM's light blinked as she broke in like a calm deity above the furore.

"Connection with Joshua has been lost. Do you request I retry?"

Holly shook her head as if the messenger could see.

"No, PAM, please try Farlow."

There was a pause, during which the green light blinked repeatedly then Laura returned to stand at her shoulder and stare at the scene of devastation.

"No connection with Farlow. Repeat, no connection with Farlow," PAM intoned, beyond reproach. Mother and daughter sat motionless, helpless, waiting.

Cath

She found him in the darkest corner, leaning against the bar, his long, sinewy forearms resting along the counter. He was staring, oblivious, at the rows of bottles in his view. That stillness was part of him — an impassivity that conveyed enigma and warning. It was what drew people to him in bids for recognition and to belong inside his sphere. The flickering, silver light of a screen allowed glimpses of his features; of the coarse stubble that decorated his angular jaw and the delicate tracery of web tattooed on to the shaved side of his head.

Cath shrank back further into the recess. She knew so little about his past, despite their having lived together for three years. Once he'd recounted a story that his grandfather had campaigned in the African wars and had been massacred in an ambush before he was born, but she could never gauge how many of his anecdotes were true. His family had been from Ireland but he refused to divulge details of his mother, merely telling her he'd left home as soon as was able, in his teens. But what had he done? How had he lived and supported himself? She'd asked, and received a shrugged 'this and that' in reply, signifying an end to her enquiries.

That he harboured a veiled cruelty, a callousness, was something she was aware of. It was one of the more disquieting elements of their relationship, but also a quality that elevated him, added to his mystique and allure. She thrust it down inside her, this knowledge, although it pulled her to him like a trap.

Images hovered in the light above the bar, a reporter in a bio-suit gesturing at the scene behind him, a tent screening the subject, its pale fabric billowing in the breeze. The monitor panned closer, moving to the ground. There was an abrupt cut to one of the smaller bodies; wet, matted fur, dark patches of red, a gaping mouth revealing spikes of teeth below eyes like marbles — wide open and vacant. Last night, a snarling, slavering killing machine, today an inert, bloody corpse. Cath felt a pang of sympathy. After all, hadn't it performed the task it was raised for? It certainly hadn't asked for the job. The monitor swung back to reveal more dead dogs strewn around the tent, felled where they'd attacked, extinguished doing their duty. She shuddered, trying to imagine how that other body looked, now removed for forensic examination — as if anyone could doubt the cause of death! It was said he'd been eviscerated, that his face was absent, although gossip travelled fast through the re-loke community.

She stepped out of the shadows and up behind his shoulder.

"OK, doll?"

The words slid from the corner of his mouth,

74

though he'd not shifted and continued to focus on the same spot behind the bar. She perched on a stool between him and the hovering pictures. The news had moved on to some statistics about food prices.

"Drink?"

She asked for a wine, aware that not to do so would appear joyless, an attitude he frowned upon. He signalled Reub, the barman with his minimal gesture of upturned finger. Reub smiled at her.

"All right, Cath?"

She waited while her glass of fabricated 'Merlot-style' was placed on the counter then took a small sip. The dribble of smooth liquid slid down her throat leaving a slight metallic taste. She felt her shoulders tense.

"I think my sister, Laura, will be in a bad state. They will all be. I feel I should go up there to them and offer some help."

She paused. It was unwise to say too much, to 'prattle on' as he called it. She didn't think her sister needed help; she knew it. She hadn't mentioned the meet she'd made with her sister last night, when Laura had refused to be drawn, had sat in a chair, ashen faced and tight-lipped, a tremor in her voice and her fingers pulling constantly on a tissue caught between them. "It could have been Josh, or Holly," she'd sobbed as a fresh batch of tears emerged and flooded down her cheeks.

Cath had cast around for some words, some phrase to comfort or console. If she'd really been there instead of an image, she'd have reached her arms around her sister and hugged her. She was unused to assuming a maternal attitude towards her, having always been the feckless, wayward sibling. Despite being the younger child, it had fallen to Laura to become the sensible, hard-working, steady one as well as counsellor, supporter and often critic of her older sister. Now Cath was at a loss to understand how she could help. She had only been back in her home town for a few weeks and was, as yet, unsure of the welcome her estranged family might give her.

"Shall I come up?" She faltered. "I'm sure I could get a pass. Spider can get anything like that. Times like this — family should stick together." The words were tumbling out in a rush, unprepared and unwanted. Laura stared into the air in front of her as if she'd forgotten she was there.

"You won't be allowed through the cordon. We are in a lockdown. It's a crime scene, Cath, besides the bio-issues such as disease control. We can't take the risk. And nobody else knows you're there in Longhope; I haven't mentioned your relocation yet — not to Josh and not to Dad either."

So she still hadn't told them, hadn't begun to negotiate for her sister's return to the family. Cath sensed all the old feelings of injustice welling and looked away as she attempted to thrust them down, lock them back into distant memory where they belonged. 'Superior even in the depths of your misery' was what

Cath wanted to say.

"What can I do?" she whispered.

Laura looked down at the shreds of tissue in her lap, her hair falling lank and tangled across her face. "You are in a position to find out who might have come up here yesterday, Cath."

There was the censorial tone she knew so well, fraying any familial bonds, broadening the rift that existed between them; she, the rebellious, unconventional risk-taker, entering into ill-advised relationships with wasters and philanderers and one short-lived marriage. Laura, the serious, diligent achiever, towing the line and gaining financial security before marrying brilliant, stable, sorted Joshua and giving birth to child prodigy, Holly. No wonder they were blessed with every advantage, like the family farm perched safe on a dry hillside away from encroaching seas and incipient, creeping floods.

She'd been so excited when their relocation application had been accepted, feeling a sense of coming home — not quite to the farm, the solid stone Welsh house she'd been brought up in, but near enough to feel she was back under the umbrella of the family. She'd had high hopes, especially for Jack, who might have benefited from the family influence and even make some kind of relationship with Hugh. All this might have been possible if not for him — Spider.

He snorted and lifted his glass to throw back a mouthful of fabricated beer. 'Authentic hoppy taste,' it would state on the carton.

"Your sister," he turned to her, the lines around his eyes creased with amusement. "She's bound to make a drama out of it. You can't go up there, Cath. The cops will be swarming all over it like bacteria. There'll be no one in or out. There's nothing you can do anyway. And from what you've said it doesn't seem like they want you. You're better off down here. You've got a good job. No point in giving it up."

She blinked and drank some more wine to camouflage her response. Being used to his cold-hearted comments did nothing to alleviate the hurt they caused her, especially when they were applied to someone close to her, like a family member.

"I could do the practical things, like housekeeping. They'll be short-handed now. Laura will have to take over a lot more work with him" — she paused, "gone. I could do washing, cleaning, making meals, looking after Holly."

His eyes narrowed as he straightened. "We've got a kid too, remember? Who's going to look after him? Not yours truly, for a start."

No. It was a given. He would never take any responsibility for Jack, the encumbrance, the baggage. The child was tolerated, for now, but fatherhood was not on Spider's agenda, nor ever had been. It was a situation Cath accepted, knowing that Jack himself was the one to have made a sacrifice, not having had a choice.

She watched as Reub loaded bags of snacks into a

dispenser, thinking for the umpteenth time how beautiful he was, a smooth black cherub with his baby-faced features and muscular torso. He looked after himself, working out most days in the block gym, one of the few who took advantage of the facility.

Reuben

The Submariner bar rested on pylons driven into the lagoon bed, the remainder of the prefabricated tower block piled on its head, resting, for the main part above the water line, although water had begun to lap at the windows of the, now vacated, first floor of apartments. Here, below the water there was no vestige of the rain or gales raging above, so it retained a cosy, snug atmosphere redolent of a bygone age.

In a jocular nod to its situation, the walls were adorned with jaunty portholes showing vids depicting aquatic life. You could enjoy your Fab pint or your TT whisky and look out on a riot of colourful coral, a forest of tall kelp housing parrot, clown and angel fish, the translucent balloons of jellyfish or a lugubrious octopus.

Reub surveyed the circular images as he stood polishing glasses. That the seascapes presented no aspect of the scene beneath the lagoon was appropriate, he always thought, since not one aspect of the Submariner was the genuine article; not the beer, the wine, the food or, he considered, the clientele, most of whom were involved in activities that were, at best, unethical — most decidedly illegal.

The majority of patrons of The Sub hailed from the

lagoon estate — re-lokes, most of them. They were the underprivileged, those who'd had no means to provide themselves with a new home like the inhabitants of the pontoon mansions nestling in the bay.

Reub's messenger console bleeped, wrenching him from his thoughts.

"It's Maynard," PAM informed him.

"Hello, darling."

"How's your afternoon, love?"

Reub grinned at the image of his partner of ten years, his face full of ill-matched features, the over large mouth, long nose and protuberant eyes. It had never been a handsome face yet portrayed a character brimming with charm and warmth.

"We have a visitor, hon."

"Jack?"

"Yes. Darling, can you bring something nice back with you when you finish your shift?"

"What, like a gorgeous, swarthy port worker?"

Maynard laughed his deep, throaty chuckle. "Now wouldn't that be fun! No dear, something our young man might like to eat. You know the kind of thing; chem-burger or pizza."

Reub pouted. "He'd be better off with a healthy meal we put together. We could do a tofu Chinese."

Maynard assumed an air of patient superiority. "Nine-year-old boys don't go for healthy vegetable matter, Reuben."

"All right. I'll see what I can find at the Depot.

What's he doing now?"

"He's watching the news bulletin. This killing bothers him, Reub, what with it involving some girl in his class at school. He keeps asking about the dogs; 'what was it like?' — that kind of thing."

Reub frowned. "Distract him with a game?"

"I've tried that but he isn't interested — just wants to know every detail. Says his school friend was there when it happened. He wants to go up there and see."

"They won't allow anyone up there, May, you know that. Just keep him happy until I get home and we'll find an activity to amuse him. See you later."

He turned to check his reflection in the mirrored wall behind the bar, stooping to brush a hand through his dark hair and glowering at the few strands of white that peppered it here and there. Overall, his appearance pleased him. He was proud of his brown, flawless skin and the clean line of his jaw, unmarred as yet by unsightly folds. As soon as any blemish, line or flap of unwanted flesh appeared he'd promised himself to get it fixed.

In the couple's re-loke apartment, Jack sat mesmerised on the edge of the sofa, staring at the scene, motionless even as Maynard placed a bowl of Ringos within his reach before sitting beside him.

"Reuben's bringing dinner, sweetie. Did you message your Ma yet? She needs to know where you are."

The boy continued to sit transfixed, his long, dark

eyelashes unblinking, straight hair lank over the neck of his sweatshirt. He had the pale, pinched look of a child neglected, like a baby bird trampled by its siblings in a bid for attention. Maynard wanted to fold him up in his arms in as near as he could get to a maternal embrace but knew the gesture could so easily be misconstrued.

Jack

Jack Pewsey ran up the five floors of fire escape steps and skittered along the tenement balcony, wet and blustery in the gathering storm. He skidded to a halt at the apartment door, placing his hand flat on the pad and hearing the faint click as the palm recognition responded, flicking damp strands of unkempt hair from his eyes as he entered the lobby. From the family room the sounds of the media console drifted out, familiar yet indecipherable; some stupid soap serial or an ancient sitcom. He let the door close with a soft click before slipping his feet from his trainers and treading softly past the closed living room towards his bedroom, almost gaining the sanctuary of it before the voice assaulted his ears.

"Oh, so you do live here then, do you? What happened? Get hungry or something?"

Ignoring the hectoring words, the boy continued on into his room, leaving the door and crossing to where the message centre blinked its red eye in an unwavering accusation. Behind him Cath stood in the doorway, as detectable by the rank smell of illicit, stale tobacco as by the rasping cough that was her constant companion. He kept his back to her as he pressed the message button, breathing life into the wall screen opposite his bed. It flickered for an instant before PAM's voice filled the room.

"Hello, Jack. Mrs Philips needs to speak to you."

He glanced quickly at Cath, accustomed to the narrowed eyes and thin lips for their 'told you so' expression.

Mrs Philips's calm, smiling presence filled the small bedroom, imbuing Jack with an embarrassed flush as he squirmed under her countenance, despite it being a recording. A barrage of rain-filled gusts was assaulting the small window and shuddering tremors were beginning to wrack the building as it rocked on its stilts.

"It's good to make contact with you, Jack."

He winced. It was this very reasonableness that caused his discomfort. He wished she would shout or threaten him, both of which behaviours he was used to from Spider and Cath, but his teacher retained her unerring, rational, level headed demeanour whatever he had or had not done.

"We missed you for our screen conference sessions today, but you can catch up on the lessons and there's still time to do your mathematics assignment and submit it before the deadline." She began to explain how to access the links to the day's lessons and how he could access help if he needed it but was cut off in an abrupt curtailment of her explanation as he flicked the switch to off. The buffeting and stormy gusts were becoming stronger. He moved to the window. Outside, the waters of the small harbour were becoming choppy, causing the moored vessels to buck and jostle against their berths. Vestiges of home-made placards and signs were still evident as strewn planks and sheets, blowing about on the quayside or lodged against fences or piles of pallets.

"Where's my Dad?" he asked Cath, keeping his back to her.

"He'll be back later. You need to speak to your teacher, Jack. You need your schooling. What do you think you're going to do without any education, without qualifications? And you know what will happen? They'll stop our coupons; maybe even chuck us out of the social housing when they get on to you."

The boy shrugged his narrow shoulders, still staring from the window as the billowing clouds of rain surged across in bulging waves, hitting the window glass in violent spatters before collecting together in rivulets and running down.

"There's a girl in my class — Holly. Her mum and dad have got a food farm. It was raided. A man was killed. The security dogs got him. They tore him to bits, tore his face off so you couldn't recognise him. It was a man that worked there."

Cath leaned back against the door frame and crossed her arms and she narrowed her eyes.

"Who told you that, Jack?"

"A mate told me. But everyone down there knew;

everyone in the protest." He'd turned to face her now and jerked his head in the direction of the window as he spoke. "The farmer, Holly's dad, that is, he had to shoot all the dogs but he was too late to save the bloke who worked there. A lot of people are saying it's the protesters carrying out the raids. When they're caught, they'll get deported. That's what Harp says."

Cath frowned at the boy. Somehow, she'd lost all control or influence over him and now he ran with a pack of older, wilder, worldlier and more cynical individuals. She feared for him as he blundered on through his young life, choosing one wrong path after another to follow.

"We don't know that any of it is true; whether it even happened. They might put a story like that about to discredit the protest, so it seems like they're a bunch of murdering thieves. In any case you shouldn't be out with the likes of Harper Duffy. He's a lot older than you and his lot are never going to make anything of themselves. You need to be getting on with your school work, conferencing with them and your teacher and going to your class v-meets like everyone else your age."

"It might be right though. What if it is? It could have been him, couldn't it? It could have been Spider and his lot. Where does he get the stuff he comes home with? Not from the community stores, is it? They don't have any of that stuff there. They don't have fresh fruit and vegetables, not that I've seen. We never get fresh apples with our vouchers. He's always coming home with stuff you don't see in the store, like raspberries or tomatoes. Where does he get it from?"

The fury that welled up inside Cath's chest was part fuelled by her own, private doubts concerning the man she called her partner; the man with whom she'd thrown in her lot in the rush of flattered, grateful mistaken-for-love zeal. How long ago now? Jack had been just three years old, when she'd had to take on the role of his stepmother, barely old enough to remember his feckless, unreliable mother. She herself had swapped a spineless, ineffectual lover for an enigmatic man she knew little more about now than she did when they met. His air of mystery had been part of the attraction, that and the aura of power and authority he exuded; his utter conviction in his ability to buck the system, to overturn the establishment. Though she might argue his innocence in any incursion she would shelter a nagging doubt that was difficult to ignore and manifested in vehement denial.

"You know where our extra supplies come from," she argued. "He's got contact-traders and port workers. He does favours for people and they pay him in goods. That's how it works. I don't see you complaining when we get a piece of meat or some real butter. It's mostly stuff that's meant to go to those at the top; people who can pay. Sometimes it gets damaged or contaminated then we get to have it."

The boy rolled his eyes, knowing beyond his nine

years.

"Knocked off is what you mean."

She walked across to share his view. The small window gave out on to a panorama of the harbour with its bobbing pontoon quays, warehouses, containers and moored vessels. Beyond this industrious scene lay the grey waters of the channel, white tipped and choppy, throwing up flecks of foam that flew like spit over the apartment blocks and landed in bubbly dollops on the landings and in the open stairwells. Along the undulating platforms loaded pallets were lined up, awaiting despatch with their stacks of sealed boxes containing goods for export. To the uninitiated these piles of waiting items looked vulnerable, looked like easy prey for port thieves and chancers, but surveillance was tight, as a cursory glance along the port authority buildings affirmed. Every few metres a camera panned from side to side surveying the entire stock, backed up by regular drone air patrols relaying footage to the security office.

Years ago, there had been vast harbours around the world using giant cranes and hoists that lifted thousands of containers on to huge, motorised ships. But they'd become too huge, too unwieldy, too expensive and too polluting. Nowadays almost all goods and commodities could be manufactured and grown at home, rendering such a massive scale of commerce unnecessary and undesirable. Import and export had become a smaller, more domestic exercise and only small amounts of goods needed to be shipped from one area to another. Vessels, equipment and ports were worked on a relatively miniature scale, and new, small village harbours were being created constantly as water levels continued to rise.

Jack and Cath watched as a tall figure, coat collar up and bent against the wind, emerged from the side of a warehouse, walked across to a pontoon, took a small item from his lips and flicked it into the lapping water before turning towards their block, shoulders hunched and hands thrust into his pockets. Spider. Jack turned from the window and sat down at the console.

"I'll have a look at what she wants us to do," he told Cath.

She took her cue and withdrew. "We'll be eating in about an hour so don't go out again." She pulled the door closed as she left him. Moments later she heard steel tipped boots clanging on the stairs then Spider was filling the tiny hallway with his presence, the chipped door opened behind him as he pulled a large carton in from the landing. Standing to face him she stared down at the carton and up into his narrow, wizened face, the question clear, in her expression.

"I picked up a few bits. It's nothing special; just thought we could do with some extras."

She knew better than to ask where it came from or how it had seemed to teleport up to their floor, when he'd crossed the wharf below them empty handed. He moved past her and on into the cramped, untidy space that was the kitchen, carrying the box and placing it on top of the hob which provided the only clear surface.

"Want to see what I got you?"

She sighed. He was always like this; always turning up with items 'for her' as if she were foremost in his mind when he was out conducting what he termed 'business'. It was his way of keeping her at heel, she knew; his method of keeping a roof over his head and his child cared for. She followed him and watched as he unpacked the contents of the box, holding each item aloft for her to exclaim over. There were two packs of chem-beef, a bag of fresh mushrooms, a bunch of carrots and something rolled up in recycled plastic wrap. She reached in and withdrew the packet, unravelling it and staring at the contents.

"Meat!"

He sniggered, watching her.

"What sort is it?"

Greenergy Longhope

Berensen sat opposite Josh across the wide, polished space of his desk. He was leaning back regarding the opposite wall where an old-style map of the world hung. Josh had studied this map countless times while on previous visits, fascinated by the way the land masses looked back then. How must it have been? So much solid land! And snow and ice in the north and the south! Now he ignored it to concentrate on the eyes of the Greenergy executive — guileless eyes in the broad, smooth face of one who lived a comfortable, privileged existence.

Berensen was speaking in calm, measured tones — as well he could, having experienced no loss.

"It was only going to be a matter of time before something like this happened. You might say we've all been lucky so far. You've lost a man, I know, but elsewhere it's been far worse — whole outfits laid to siege, many workers lost, many millions in profit wasted."

'You've lost a man'. He made it sound as if Josh had been careless, dropped an object from his pocket or failed to maintain a piece of machinery.

"They were like a part of our family, Farlow and

Ewa! Farlow wasn't just an employee! He was like my brother. We've been ripped apart, man — just as he was…" He faltered. 'Just as his body was torn limb from limb,' he'd meant to say. The pictures in his head tortured him day and night like some demonic carousel revolving; the noises, the howling, raging wind, the snarling, snapping animals, the near-human screams of them tearing into the man; his yelping, gasping cries as they set about him, the feverish, pungent stench of terror mingled with blood. Josh felt his gorge rise and swallowed quickly, becoming aware of Berenson's voice, compelling in its composure.

The man opposite continued as if uninterrupted, his blue eyes unwavering from the spot above Josh's head. 'Almost as if he were PAM' was what Josh thought, as Berenson droned on.

"You've no need to struggle on now, Josh, you and your family. You can get all the help you need. I know it's a difficult time for you — you, Laura and little Holly, but I want you to think again about coming under the Greenergy umbrella, into *our* extended family, so to speak. You would see the benefits immediately. All your bio-controls, plant nutrition, infrastructure, maintenance; everything would be supplied by us. Your role need not change. You would be overall manager just as you are at present. Perhaps Laura might like to join the fold, too?" He paused to glance down and gauge the effect his words were having, catching the look of blank incomprehension and outrage on Josh's face.

"Let me get this right, Berenson. The day after we suffer an event that robs us of our closest friend, someone who was the nearest thing to a brother to me and an uncle to Holly, you offer to buy us out, to take from us our family farm that has been in my wife's family for generations?"

The older man shrugged and bent forward, placing his elbows on the desk, narrowing his eyes into glittering blue points like diamond cutters.

"It is a good offer." His voice was soft even as the words hit hard. "Take a little time to think it over. You wouldn't want to look back and regret any decisions made in the haste of your... reactions. You have your family's future to consider. There's young Holly. She's a bright little thing, I gather. Greenergy would take care of her education then she'd come out with a ready-made career on the counter. She'd be set up for life, never want for anything."

Josh swallowed hard. The man must be mad. He exerted enough effort to keep his voice low and even, must not reveal his anger. "I see. You would like to take my farm *and* my wife and daughter off my hands. Is there anything you don't want to relieve me of, Berenson? You haven't mentioned my father-in-law yet, or my son."

He got to his feet, pushing the chair back. Berenson waved his hands in a dismissive, placatory fashion, adopting an indulgent, avuncular smile. "Now Josh, don't be too hasty. We've had a good working relationship in the past. There's no reason why it shouldn't continue. Why don't you go and talk it over with Laura? The situation may seem different in a few days, you know, when the dust has settled."

Joshua looked down at him, a coldness seeping through his being. "You've said enough. You can consider our 'working relationship' finished." He turned his back and left the room, closing the door as quietly as his feelings would allow, conscious of little except for a pounding pulse jerking through him like a pile driver. Once he was out of the compound he glanced up. A security drone was already executing a sweep of the courtyard. The drone's sinister buzz sounded a menacing warning signal. They could hear as well as see. He decided to wait until he got home before talking to Laura. Once upon a time there were bees; gentle, benevolent and more precious than any fuel. Now there were drones; aggressive, intrusive and infinitely replaceable. You never knew what you had until it was gone.

Greenergy's tunnels stretched outwards beyond the compound, a sea of bulbous pipes in every direction reaching out towards the horizon and housing only oil seed rape. Tufts of it sprang up between the tunnels, along the margins of the compound and between the slabs paving it, as if it was set to take over the planet. Yellow-flowered oil seed rape — the resilient king of the plant world. And yet you couldn't eat it. Josh loathed the stuff, even though he depended on it to fuel his vehicles. They had to wage a permanent war on it to defend their food growing operation. In his nightmares he entered a potato tunnel to find it packed full with clouds of invading pale-yellow oil seed rape. He shuddered.

He shed his bio-suit at the entrance and located his bike. Today's rain was light, which would make repairs easier, but could still have carried disease into the polytunnels at home, where gaping holes exposed the plants.

As he neared the farm, he wondered what he could say to Laura about his meeting with Berenson. She was in a state of shock. They all were, his little family — pale, trembling ghosts who spoke in whispers and cried steady, silent tears as they went about the chores. He feared most for Holly who'd had no experience of loss and had withdrawn into herself, spending hours in her room curled on her bed, staring at the wall.

Cath

Knowing where the boy would be, for the third time that week, Cath climbed the three floors to their landing and messaged them. Hearing the door click open she stepped into the hallway — a carbon copy design of her own tiny porch except as different as an art gallery from a warehouse. They had contrived in the narrow space to create an immediate sensation of welcome in the colourful wall and floor coverings, the utilitarian plastic beneath her feet covered with a thick, fibrous rug made from recycled textiles, the limited wall space crammed with hangings, drawings, paintings, masks, appliqués and collages; Maynard's work.

She called a greeting into the apartment and was met by him as she stopped to inspect an old monochrome photograph of Longhope as it once was, a sleepy village basked in shafts of sunlight, no water in sight.

"Dear heart! Are you all right?"

She was caught up in a bear hug as he enveloped her. There was an instantaneous comfort in the fleshy mounds of his bulky girth. Since she'd been their neighbour, she'd become fonder of this couple than anyone else she'd met on the estate. They had also developed a genuine affection for Jack, who they spoiled with the merciless affection of maiden aunts. But he enjoyed the attention and it compensated in part from the austere disinterest he received from Spider.

She followed Maynard into their cosy living room which was furnished in the same, homespun style as the hall, with lavish drapes at the windows and comfortable, squashy sofas covered in hand-made throws.

The boy barely acknowledged her as she sank down next to him.

"Cup of tea, dear?" May beamed his wide grin before making a tactical withdrawal into the tiny galley kitchen.

She glanced around the room. Their own living room remained in its original, functional state, containing the minimal furniture and fixtures that had been provided when they moved into the block. She'd had such hopes for it then, even though she'd grieved for their urban flat, a deluded sense of nesting leading her to believe she and Spider would be making a new start in creating a home for themselves and Jack. But now, after two years, she'd had to face the fact that her chosen life partner had no more interest in home-making than he had in forging a career. He was only interested in their shared accommodation as a base, a place to sleep and have occasional — and if it were to be admitted, increasingly rare — sex with her. Nowadays it was a rare event for the three of them to sit down for a meal together, let alone to spend an evening in each other's company.

She watched as Jack's slender fingers reached into the bowl of Ringos on his lap, his gaze unwavering, fixed on the news images. What was his preoccupation with it all? He'd asked her repeatedly about it. 'What was it like?' It was as if some loop was running in his brain that he was unable to halt.

She touched his arm. "Coming home?"

He shook his head briefly without looking at her. "Can't I stay? Reub's bringing dinner back after his shift.'

Maynard's moon face appeared around the door. Cath left the child and went out to the minute space of the kitchen, where pans and utensils hung around the walls like a sculpture installation. Maynard cooked. In this, as in all his endeavours, he was creative, artistic, painstaking. Before, he and Reuben had kept and run an art café, its landscaped grounds backing on to The Thames river at Chiswick in south London. Diners could sit al fresco on a riverside terrace to enjoy his delicious meals. Reuben had dealt with the business side and 'front of house', sourcing fine wines and creating a luxurious, relaxing ambience. She'd seen the images, heard the story. Now it was gone, washed away on the tides of change like so much else.

They were survivors though, Maynard and Reub. They'd made the best of it. Reub had his bar work. Maynard did all right from selling his art fabricated from discarded objects.

"How's it going?" he asked her as he spooned tea into a proper teapot. She leaned her elbows on the worktop and watched him, soothed by the careful, meticulous way he undertook this simple, domestic task.

"I don't know, May. Everything seems to be falling apart. My sister isn't doing so well. The whole family is devastated. I wanted to help them; you know? But she says I shouldn't go up there. Nobody but Laura knows I'm here yet, and Spider…"

"Spider doesn't want you to go."

"No and they're going to move Ewa and Kav into the farmhouse with them."

"Well that's good, isn't it?" He looked sideways at her; bushy eyebrows raised. "That poor girl needs all the help she can get; new baby and widowed all in the space of a few weeks."

Cath nodded once, staring at the counter. "I know."

He was getting cups out, bustling, his large frame filling the miniature kitchen. "Were you hoping you and yours might get to go and live up there, was that it?"

She could only nod, swallowing, tearful. "I thought maybe we could justify our accommodation, May, you know? I'm not much good at farm work. I don't have their science backgrounds. I never applied myself at school, like Laura did. I made too many mistakes. Then there's Ethan. I regret so much, May. I want to make up for it. I could have looked after the other stuff — the home, the cooking, the laundry."

He was pouring the tea. "And get to see Ethan sometimes?"

She was silent.

"What about Spider? Where was he going to fit into your plan?" He was looking at her now, the irony plain.

"Oh, I know! He wouldn't fit into anyone's plan. He wouldn't fit anywhere. In any case she's just about said outright that we, Jack and me, can go and live there, long as Spider doesn't come. But May, she still hasn't told anyone else we are here in Longhope. She says it's too soon, that they haven't got over Mum's taking," she was gabbling now, blurting everything out like she'd been unable to with Spider. "And I never even saw Mum before they took her." Her words gave way to a shuddering sob.

He handed her a cup. "Well honey, that's good news for Reub and me. We certainly don't want you to go. How else do I get to fulfil my maternal ambitions if I can't get to see Jack every day?"

Hugh

It had not been a good time to tell them. There was never going to be a good time but now, with the change of circumstances, it was expedient. He'd already briefed Ethan, who seemed confident to help despite the trauma of his injury — even relishing the task as a way of adapting to the tech-arm he'd been given.

Outside the wind had subdued to a grumbling whine and the rain to an odd squall, smattering against the windows as if to remind them they had a reprieve, but it would be back. And it always would be, he thought, grimacing, like C S Lewis's Narnia; always winter but never Christmas.

They'd taken to eating meals together a month before he'd announced his decision, congregating around the table like wrapping a lifebelt around them, with the shared company keeping them afloat. In truth it was the baby, Kav, who, in his innocence, was keeping them together, giving them a reason to carry on. He proved both a distraction from their misery and a focus, like a beacon on which to pin their hopes for the future.

He'd mulled over his speech a thousand times, dreaming it at night, rehearsing it in his head, telling it to the struggling roses he still tried to cultivate as the sickly flowers whipped to and fro in an attempt to keep their petals in the teeth of the murderous winds. Now, with a month until his departure, he knew he'd prepared enough. He'd made his peace with his errant daughter, Cath, in an emotional v-meet, when he'd promised to do everything he could, to reunite her with the family.

He waited for a lull in the desultory talk, which consisted mainly of rotas, which jobs needed prioritising and how the finances would stretch over the next couple of weeks.

Kav whimpered a little on Ewa's lap. "He's tired," she said, gathering the baby up and standing to leave. Since the killing she'd grown thin and fragile like a spectre.

"No." Hugh stopped her. "Stay for just a few minutes with Kav. I want everyone to hear what I have to say, even if they don't understand."

He had their attention. Ewa sat down, her hand around Kav's downy head as she rocked him gently, his blond eyelashes fluttering.

"I've been trying to find a way to tell you," Hugh began, looking around the table. Their eyes were on him, Laura's mouth a little open, Josh's chin resting on his hand, Holly erect, staring at him with fierce concentration. "I've made my decision…"

"You're leaving us!" Laura cried.

"How did you know?"

She'd changed so much in the last few weeks, he

thought. She wore a weariness, a lack of commitment in the slump of her shoulders and her small frown. Traces of lines had appeared around her eyes. She went about tasks in a stoical, dogged trance, unable to conjure enthusiasm; no lively discussion over this or that insecticide, no controversial ideas for new fruits, no research into new machinery or methods. He looked away from her to his granddaughter and saw confusion in Holly's face.

"Where are you going, Granddad?"

"To North Africa; a country that was called Egypt once. I'll live in a village near the desert, close to the SOL farms. You'll be sad, for a time," he continued, focusing on the young girl, "but we will have almost as much contact as we have ever had. It just won't be physical." He watched her expression begin to alter now as the colour drained from her cheeks and some understanding dawned.

"We still need you, Hugh! We need your advice and we need your experience, your knowledge of what went before." Josh looked earnest but his chin remained on his hand.

"It's a long time since you needed me, Joshua. It's high time I left here. I must create a space for someone younger now. Laura, I want you to think about your sister and her responsibilities. I haven't been able to offer her the same chances as you've had. I want you to think about giving them a home here. Young Jack — he'll be as intelligent just as Holly here. He'll be able to learn. He just needs the chances she's getting."

Laura's head drooped, her finger moving some salt grains around the table surface. "I know we can't change your mind, Dad."

Holly's face was red now. This was a shock almost as terrible as Farlow's death. She stood, shoving her chair back with an abrupt thrust and ran from the room. Her mother's voice was weak with emotion. "But Dad! Cath and Jack don't come as a twosome, do they? I can ask her, but there's no guarantee she'll want to come."

Hugh closed his eyes, remembering his leaving, a day of angry, whipping winds and lashing showers under an iron grey ceiling of cloud. They'd gathered up to see him off, a melancholy little group trying hard to suppress their feelings, to follow his instruction to 'be happy for him'.

He was bone tired. It was years since he'd travelled anywhere and had not expected that a voyage, a road trip, the inundation of sights, sounds and smells would require such energy to process. He thought he would never forget the long approach to the dock side at Alexandria, past semi-sunken, rusting hulks of vessels, their skeletal structures reaching out of the water like wraiths, the cool mist of dawn lifting like a wedding veil. As the quayside drew nearer, he was able to make out bustling figures, many draped in long robes and there were animals. Animals! His pulse raced. There were donkeys and even camels along the quay. He turned towards Ethan, who grinned to see the excitement on his grandfather's face.

But there was sadness too, in this arrival. While they'd still be in touch by PAM, this was the last real physical contact Hugh would have with any member of his family, on this earth at least.

"The bearers will be waiting," Ethan told him. "They'll be expecting you."

And there would be others, of course. He'd been consumed by the thought of his new life for so long he considered it more of a rebirth than a slide into extinction.

As Ethan, expert even with his handicap, slid Futura into her mooring Hugh looked up. The sky was a livid, blood crimson, the air already warm and filled with a thousand scents; everything from bio-fuel to human sweat, from animal excrement to exotic fruit. He gazed around as the boat was made secure. In the full light of day, the dockside was a visual feast, teeming with porters, passengers, luggage, animals, cargo and sailors. He felt a momentary tremor of anxiety. How would he find his transport? But Ethan seemed calm; he'd completed this passage many times and would know what to do.

He put down his small bag and sat down to wait, watching as an olive-skinned mule-driver loaded his cart, clambering on top to load it to twice its height. It seemed an impossible load for the animal to haul. The beast's ribs stood out like a concertina and its haunches protruded in sharp angles but the driver leapt down from the load, where he'd been securing it, climbed into the seat and flicked a slender whip over the mule's back, at which it started forward, head down. Hugh tracked its progress as the cart wore its way through the throng, catching glimpses of the driver's green robe and his scarlet turban until at last they disappeared.

"It's time, Hugh." Ethan had his bag and was ready to disembark. The elderly man followed his grandson down the gangway and on to the quay. Africa! The sights, sounds and smells crowded in on him as he followed the straight-backed young man down the gangway, experiencing a swooning of heat from the paved jetty as he stepped on to it. Here was a tall, pouting camel, still as a sculpture inside its cart shafts, small boys in loose shifts dodging through the spice stalls, boxes piled into mountains of riotous shades, umber, scarlet, bronze and yellow.

They wove their way through the crowd to the end of the quay and across a market square humming with commerce then on to a concourse where several large transport vehicles were lined up. By now, Hugh was sweating as the sun rose higher and was glad of the large-brimmed hat Ethan had supplied him with. The lad turned to inspect him. "All right?"

He nodded. "But I've forgotten how the sun feels. I haven't felt this warm outside since I was a child."

Ethan grinned. "Isn't that part of the reason you came?"

"Some," he mumbled. They were standing by a

long vehicle with windows along the sides; a bus. Glancing up, Hugh could see the faces of other passengers already on board. Ethan placed his bag into an open stowage compartment beneath the windows. "You'll be fine, Granddad. They'll take the best care of you. I have to get back to Futura if I am to meet my schedule. The tide won't wait!"

No. The tide won't wait. There was so much that was beyond the control of humankind; and so much that should have been left uncontrolled. He swallowed, wracked now as he struggled for some dignity amid his distress then allowing the tears to come as Ethan pulled him into an embrace. He sensed the muscular strength of this powerful young man and was aware of his own creeping frailty.

"Go on Granddad," he whispered, "they're waiting for you." The lad pressed him gently away, turned and plunged into the melee. 'Granddad', he'd called him. Hugh looked back at the spot where he'd left him, where the seething crowd had closed behind him like a curtain. He took a breath and climbed up into the bus.

The smiling guide welcomed him with a small bow, his palms pushed together in greeting. He did his best to reciprocate before locating his place, gaining encouraging nods and smiles from his fellow passengers as he shuffled down the middle of the vehicle. He dropped into the seat. It was cool here inside. The guide, Ahmed, began to speak.

"My friends," he paused, scanning the attentive

faces like a professor addressing his students, "you have all made the momentous first step since choosing to make this journey. I congratulate you! Now the adventure begins!" His voice, cultured and tinged with a hint of accent, was even, melodic. "You must not think of this journey in terms of what you have lost, the friends and family you will no longer touch, but as new life beginning, a new family. You will feel sad sometimes perhaps, but in time you will adjust, achieve contentment. You must feel proud of your bravery and I promise you will not be disappointed!"

His age, thought Hugh, was impossible to determine and although his dark skin was lined like tree bark and beard white, his eyes were clear and penetrating, his back unbowed.

A young boy walked down the central aisle with a tray, distributing water. Ahmed explained that they would be travelling for a couple of hours before stopping for a break and something to eat at a settlement. Some guests would be leaving the transport here as this first village would be their new home.

Hugh leaned back, sighing. He had an empty seat next to him. They all did. There was more than enough time to get to know new friends but, for now, the guide was aware that each of them needed to be alone with their emotions, to begin to make the adjustment. He closed his eyes.

"Dad still needs you! He told you!"

He'd hugged her close, feeling the imprint of her

slight frame, willing the feeling into his bones so that he might recreate it in the years to come. "Your Dad is a good man, but he knows I must go. There is nothing more I can do here, Holly, and I must make way for others — the next generation: you! You know this. Where I am headed, they have made a specialism of keeping old people like me alive, fit and healthy, at a time when there are too many people on the planet and nowhere near enough land to feed or house them all. You know the choice — a short span here with you or whatever time I have left there, with the sun on my back."

Their bus glided through the city streets, its solar engine producing no more than a whisper. Traffic consisted of an exotic assortment of solar, human or animal powered vehicles. There were fascinating spectacles in all directions — a colourful water-bearer, the precious calabash resting on her head, stalls selling unrecognisable foods, implements or clothing, repair shops, street food stalls.

At last the commercial premises petered out and gave way to residential areas — low, white boxes of dwellings with mere slits for windows; to be cool, Hugh supposed. Eventually the houses themselves became sparser as the bus turned on to a bare, dusty road that led into the desert. Here were only rocks, sand and sky. He had never seen a landscape so barren, without a speck of green, so light without a puff of cloud, so sterile or so beautiful.

Cath

Cath glanced at the woman seated in the image, recognising defeat in the sag of her shoulders, the drawn features and the dull tone of her voice as she told her story. Each client was convinced their story was new and yet it was a tale she'd heard hundreds of times. But the woman still needed to tell it, to unload some of the misery. Cath sat back in her chair, her practised, sympathetic nod signalling the woman to go ahead — tell.

They'd sunk everything they had into their dream home, she said. They'd been so thrilled when they'd saved enough for their deposit. They were only twelve years away from paying back the loan. It was so beautiful, overlooking the water meadows. Her boy had been so happy there.

Cath nodded and composed her face into an empathetic smile, recalling Maynard's words to her.

"We're the lucky ones, Cath. We've been relocated. We have a roof over our heads. Life is what we make it, not how it's made for us."

She suppressed a sigh as the woman continued, pulling at the lapel of her jacket with nervous fingers. It was good quality, Cath noted. Whatever belongings she had lost it must have been purchased from the one of the best stores and didn't appear to be an up-cycled garment.

She had ground to a halt in the story of her family's misfortunes. Her eyes, lugubrious tinged with a glint of anticipation, lifted to meet Cath's. She and her husband and son were residing currently in the holding centre, sharing the large, warehouse dormitory with twenty other families and using the communal kitchen. Now she sat in the centre's tiny cupboard of a message room to take her turn.

Cath donned her bright, efficient smile. "Well, Mrs Arthur, the news is good."

Mrs Arthur sat upright and lurched forward, eyes wide. "You have a house for us?" she gasped. Cath's smile tempered to moderate. She placed her elbows on the desk. "You have to remember, Mrs Arthur, that we are the lucky ones. We get to have a roof over our heads. I'm afraid there are simply no actual houses for the folks who need to be relocated, at least, not unless they are able to fund the property themselves, but I can offer you a very nice, clean, comfortable and dry, two-bedroom apartment."

The woman stared at her, bottom lip quivering, fingers clutching her cheek. "Our home was beautiful, *beautiful* — you understand? We had four bedrooms. Four! All with views of the water meadows. Lewis loved it. We had a garden with a swing and a climbing frame. He had a football goal net, a trampoline…"

Cath interrupted. "Yes Mrs Arthur. I can imagine how lovely it was." She smiled again, though impatience was creeping in. "We have all been relocated here because we lost our homes. We have earned the right to this home here by possessing a skill, a qualification or experience that enables us to work here. I, myself, have an apartment here. I have it because I worked as a housing officer back in the South East, which is now, like your lovely home, under water. Most people settle well once they've adjusted to the change and make the most of their apartments. You'll be surprised how cosy and pleasant they can be. I have a good friend who could help you with that." She had the fleeting thought that they, she, Spider and Jack, had not put Maynard's services to use in their living space. Why was this? She continued with a warning to the woman. "I must tell you that if you reject this flat, we have nothing else to offer and there is an endless queue of others in the same situation as yours, or worse, who would snap my hand off for your apartment home." She stopped, aware that she was coming across as intolerant, a quality she always strove to quash.

The woman appeared to have shrivelled, shrunk into the corner of her seat, her hands now still. She gave a faint nod as if seeing her predicament for the first time with clarity. Her voice, when she finally spoke was small, remote. "We'll take it."

"Good!" Cath sensed her own body relax. "I gather you will be joining the dock vehicles maintenance team, is that correct?"

She nodded.

"And what does your partner propose to do, Mrs Arthur?" Her shrug was barely perceptible as she picked at an invisible spot on her skirt. Cath leaned towards her image in a gesture of encouragement. "What did he do before?"

"He was a midwife in a birthing centre. He loved his job, loved it there." There was a degree of pride in her voice now, less faltering and she raised her head a little, tilting her chin. Cath made an expansive gesture. "We have our own birthing centre here in Longhope. I don't know if there are any vacancies but I can find out. And what about your little boy, Lewis?" She consulted the screen as she spoke. "You will need to register him for school here. You'll be able to do it on PAM as soon as you move in. The school is very good. My niece is registered there. Their distance learning programmes get excellent results. How does Wednesday sound for your move? The apartment should be ready by then."

"Yes. Wednesday. Thank you." Mrs Arthur sounded, Cath felt, like a beaten woman, but she had managed to thank her. Perhaps by Wednesday she'd have rallied and be a little more resigned to her situation.

She took a break, rubbing her neck and closing her eyes before the next interview. She felt like a worn mattress, existing to soften their aching losses at leaving their homes and their communities. She also felt guilty.

Who was she to be asking what the woman's husband's occupation was? She, Spider and Jack had been the beneficiaries of an apartment based solely on her abilities and contacts as a housing officer. In recent months the criteria for claiming accommodation had been reset into much stricter requirements that meant both partners must have earning power, be contributors.

If anyone had asked her what Spider did, she would be at a loss to explain. What exactly did he do? Her sister had asked this same question during one of their early v-meets when they were newly arrived to Longhope, a conversation that had felt like an interrogation, as they so often did these days. She'd stood up for him, of course. "He is an activist!" she'd cried, indignant at any implication of waster, replying as if this title justified his existence. "An eco-warrior and environmentalist! He cares about what's happening to society, Laura, and he champions the rights of ordinary people. It's OK for you. You don't understand what food poverty feels like, or homelessness."

But Laura had cut her short, making her irritation plain. "Cath, activism doesn't put food on your table, does it? And I don't see how you can criticise us for working the farm when we are doing *our* damndest to produce food for everyone!"

Cath sighed, sat up and clicked for the next number, the next traumatised, emotionally damaged re-loke on her list.

Later, as she reviewed the clients and made her

diary entries, she heard the voice-activated entry to the flat operating and then voices in the hallway. Spider had brought a visitor. She looked up when they came in.

"How are you doing?" He threw himself down on the sofa, indicating that his companion should do the same, a large, soft man, dark skinned and with a mass of Afro-style hair. He had several piercings dotted about his face and was dressed in black shirt and jeans, the jeans having that stretched look from having to cover substantial thighs, and when he leaned forward a gap between the shirt and jeans revealed the cleft at the top of his buttocks.

"This is Porc. Porc — Cath. Cath — Porc. Cath's my missus. Fancy making us a couple of teas, Doll?" He winked at her, grinning, the creases deep at the corners of his eyes. The two were beginning to pore over something they'd placed on the coffee table. It actually looked like a document made of paper, a relic, perhaps from a museum archive. Spider turned his back. She had the feeling the tea was more a ploy to get rid of her than a desire for refreshment. She ignored the request.

"Is Jack with you?" she asked, after nodding to the guest. Spider shrugged, Jack's whereabouts sparking no interest in him.

"I don't know where he is. Maybe he's in his room." He turned back to the document; the question having passed by him without consideration.

She rose and went to open Jack's door. The poky space was a mess of clothes and random items he'd picked up around the docks; packaging cartons, pieces of vehicle, on a small desk a bird's skull, bleached white in the acid waters. The message light below his screen blinked on and off in an unceasing, patient rebuke, strobing the tiny room which was empty of its occupant. On his narrow bunk a heap of jumbled bedding formed a small mountain adorned with odd socks, pyjamas and an empty Ringos packet.

She messaged him. "Jack — where are you? Come home now please. It will soon be dark and it's nearly dinner time." It wasn't dinner time. Nobody had begun to consider meal making but she needed to get a grip, to exert some control over the boy. She messaged Maynard, who was unable to respond right now. Presumably Reuben was off shift.

A yellow corner protruded from the bedding pile, another empty packet perhaps. She should get in here and clean everything up. Jack would hate it. He hated things to be clean and tidy. It was why he loved May and Reub's flat with its crowded ledges, crammed walls, overstuffed furniture and riotous objects competing for space.

She withdrew the crumpled, yellow item. It was paper, like the document next door. More paper. She began to read the text. She frowned. Why would Jack have this? It made no sense.

Hugh

The bus had stopped in a village. For a moment Hugh wondered where he was, disorientated from sleep. From the window he saw a row of low, boxy houses as before. Along the side of the track a few tiny, naked children played in the dust, scraping channels with sticks, some shrieking with laughter, some absorbed in the activity. Some scruffy hens strutted amongst them, pecking here and there although there must be little to warrant the search in the pale dust.

The driver had jumped down and was taking bags from the luggage compartment below Hugh's seat as Ahmed stood to speak again.

"My friends, we have reached our first destination — the village that is to be home for some of you." He consulted his wrist console. "In a few minutes your mentor will arrive to show you your accommodation, provide some refreshment and explain a few details to help you in your first weeks. We know you will be very happy here as you set out on this new and exciting phase of your lives. Thank you for travelling with us and we wish you good fortune in this, your next adventure!" He beamed across all their heads before calling the names on his list. "Elders Eli, Hanna, Trent and Jon, please make your way outside where your guide is waiting."

Hugh watched as three men and one woman rose from their seats to file down the centre and down the steps, their expressions eager. The remaining passengers murmured subdued encouragement as they passed. *'Be happy'*, *'Good luck'* or *'See you again'*, the latter being a mere figure of speech. He knew from his research that there were always far more men than women. Women found it more difficult to cut loose from their families, opting to shorten their lives and stay in familiar surroundings until their time came.

The four stepped out and down on to the dust verge, squinting in the strong sunlight. Two village representatives were making their way towards the bus, smiling and bowing. They all clasped hands then the four were motioned to follow. They seemed to straighten and square their shoulders, preparing to fit through this unknown doorway as they set off carrying their small bags into this next chapter of their lives. 'The final chapter', Hugh thought.

In the weeks that followed he spent many v-meet hours with Holly, showing her his home in the village. She was charmed by the colourful interior, the woven mats on the floor and the wall hangings, the tiny slots of windows that allowed narrow shafts of light to make bright stripes on the floor and walls. He showed her the garden where he was trying to coax rows of vegetables to grow, a gaggle of small, grinning children in loose smocks, their feet bare, helping him. Some held small buckets; some clutched trowels. They chattered and laughed as they dug or watered in the dusty plot. He looked happier than he had for months, her grandfather. She was glad for him.

After a month or so the v-meets became less frequent and she supposed that his new life took up more time. He was busy. It was working out well; but she missed him. They'd spent a lot of time together in his last weeks at the farm; time he'd used to imprint her mind with memories as well as exacting promises from her regarding the future.

"I know you will be sad; sadder than ever. But the world is changing so fast now and your role will be vital in influencing the impact of these changes. You will become someone special, a scientist or a politician perhaps. So much has been lost but so much can be saved if people like you stand up and speak for it! Remember Holly, your education — that is the key to everything. You have done a brilliant job so far. Keep it up, whatever happens!"

"What about you, Granddad? What will you do? I'll have no one to help me with my school projects!" Her lip trembled as she dipped her head to hide her distress.

"You can still meet with me, my love. I'll only be at wrist length away! And I will have work too, instructing about farming methods and teaching children who haven't had the benefit of an education like yours. I'll be able to show you when I'm there. Would you like that?"

She nodded once. "What will it be like there? The people you'll be living with — will they be like us?"

He thought for a moment; long enough for her to assume he didn't want to answer. "I don't know yet, Holly. You know, you can have as many v-experiences as you like but nothing is ever going to be like the real thing. I've researched the place, of course and the people there have been very helpful, but living there will be different altogether. They are ancient races, ancient tribes. They've retained some of the old ways. They still have religion. They respect elderly people which is why we older folks are welcome, if we qualify. They want our skills, our knowledge and in return they care for us as they do their own elders. It feels good to be going to a place where I can make a contribution, be needed."

Ahmed was taking Hugh out to visit a solar farm, a two-hour journey by solar powered vehicle across the desert. It was strange, Hugh considered, that the desert he'd first seen and thought so uninteresting, so devoid of features he now realised was as varied and fascinating as any landscape in the world. The vista changed from rocky outcrops in myriad colours sprouting from undulating sands to boulder-strewn plains stretching to the horizon, or sumptuous, curving dunes, silky smooth at a distance, the sand shifting visibly on occasions.

Ahmed was a comfortable travel companion, sensing when Hugh needed silence to appreciate the sights and occupying him with conversation or information when time lagged. The two had become friends, finding they had much in common despite their disparate cultures. Hugh felt fortunate to have been accommodated in Ahmed's own village and whilst the other two elders, Anders and Peter, were pleasant enough, he enjoyed the challenging discussions he had when Ahmed dropped by for tea or when they sat together at the edge of the village to watch the sunset — an event he never tired of seeing.

To an extent he was embarrassed, that he was learning more than he was imparting, though when he expressed this his friend disagreed.

"No, no, no my friend! There is no real distinction between teaching and learning. They are two points on the same circle, are they not? What better way to learn than to teach? And what better way to teach than to be constantly striving for understanding?" Ahmed was an optimist by nature as well as by religion. He challenged Hugh's view of the world as doomed.

"Why would you think this?" he demanded. "Since the beginning of mankind people have adapted, learned, made the best of what they had. This is why mankind has endured. And to be adaptable is to be optimistic. When your road is blocked you try another pathway. When he needed to eat and feed his family ancient man made tools to make it easier and learned how to grow food. When he was cold, he began to make clothes. Other ancient species did not survive. Perhaps they could not adapt or were not optimistic enough to try!"

Hugh protested. "But the poisoning and exploitation of earth's resources has itself been wrought by mankind. He has orchestrated his own downfall!"

Ahmed shook his head. "Not so, friend Hugh. It is a mere chapter in our history. Men will put the poison to some use, will find alternative resources. It happens already! What did you have too much of, back in your homeland? What was a surplus, a problem to be eradicated?"

Hugh did not hesitate. "Water! Water rising and water falling. Too much, always. Leeching the land of nutrients and forcing people from their homes."

His friend nodded. "And yet here, as you see we have none of our own at all. We could equally say our problem is sun. We have too much. This is a paradox, is it not?" He laughed, throwing his head back at the clear blue sky. "Between us we have found the solution, your people and mine. We provide your power. You provide our water. Perfect, is it not?"

Hugh grimaced. "It isn't much of a deal. Our water is poisoned with acid. Even rainwater can no longer be used untreated for irrigation or anything else. Then we create more pollution cleansing it for our own use."

"Hugh! See here, we have no shortage of a power source. It never fails. And it is all we need to purify your water. You pipe it over. We clean it. Problem solved."

When they were within half an hour of the solar farm Hugh was given a visor to wear to avoid glare damage to his eyes, his protest about deteriorating eyesight overruled. "No, no—- we have use of your eyes my friend."

In the distance a pinpoint of white light hovered near the horizon, expanding as they drew nearer. The extent of the solar field took his breath away. It was vast, stretching across the desert and disappearing into the earth's curve; a silent, recumbent country of plates, as if the entire desert had been tiled over. It was unfenced, unguarded, unpatrolled. Ahmed shrugged. "The desert is its own defence," he explained.

They travelled down a passageway between the plates, like the corridors between the polytunnels at Earthsend, until they came to some low, white buildings in the same style as his village house. A single, modest sign by the road was all there was to say that it was the property of SOL, the energy giant.

Ahmed turned to Hugh as they drove past the sign and pulled up outside the building. "Did you know, Hugh that SOL now owns and runs installations in the deserts of America, Australia and southern Europe? It is a powerful world force. I wonder what our African predecessors would think of that? Only a hundred years ago the African continent was on its knees, begging the rest of the world for help. It was decimated by corruption, wars, misguided ideology, famine, cruelty. Now it has become a world energy superpower, looked up to by everyone."

Hugh experienced a wave of despondency, as if a heavy weight had been hung around his neck. He'd expected to be freed of concepts such as 'energy superpowers' by relocating here. It was a land of purity, of high ideals; an egalitarian society that valued individuals and revered the elderly, wasn't it?

He stepped out into the blinding light and the searing heat, glad of his protective mask and clothing and to gain the cool of SOL's administration block. Following Ahmed, he entered the building to be temporarily blinded by the contrasting dark of a narrow corridor. A woman waited in an ante room.

"This is Selina, Hugh. She will show you around the installation. I'm going to see if I can find us some lunch."

Selina smiled the corporate smile and began her patter, quoting statistics; energy produced, numbers of workers, wealth achieved.

"Who do you supply?" Hugh asked. "Apart from my own homeland, of course."

Berenson

Berenson walked through his suite, stopping for a brief check of his appearance in the mirror before exiting and making his way to the restaurant. It was always good to get away for a week or two. Amongst the execs, 'recharging batteries' was a time-honoured tradition of a euphemism, especially droll in terms of the industry they worked in. None of them considered that they were privileged, since their work was essential for the continuing survival of the planet. It was this conceit that justified their lifestyles, their travel permits, their access to entertainment venues and to real, traditional protein foods such as meat.

Their hotel, a liner called Green Princess, lay at anchor somewhere in the Caribbean in a location known only to the carriers who'd ferried them there. Though not a large ship, she was furnished with every luxury and comfort, from concert halls to bars, from gymnasiums to casinos, with a vast array of activities on offer. Conference attendees could choose from a programme of traditional pursuits like diving, fishing or hunting. Their sexual desires were also considered, with sex workers providing a comprehensive range of services forming a discreet part of the provision.

Upon entering the restaurant, he located his table, at which two members were seated, conversing. One of the women, Aceline Faure, was known to him from previous conferences, the other was a newcomer. He greeted Faure. "Aceline. Good to see you again!" He turned to her companion. "And I don't believe I've had the pleasure of meeting you."

The second woman rose to shake his hand. "Uzza Farzul. I am from the former Turkey but I work near Basel. And you are Berenson? Aceline has been telling me about your successful mergers with local food producers in your area! I should like to hear more and to know what methods you use to bring the farmers into your fold!"

Berenson's opening smile was tempered, creasing only one side of his lips and not his eyes. Faure, he noticed was watching him with interest. Farzul was a gaunt, angular woman whose facial expression wore an intensity that provoked suspicion. He motioned her to sit, pulling out the chair next to Faure and settling before speaking, palms pressed together under his chin. "I'm pleased to make your acquaintance Uzza, but let's enjoy the company, the meal and these beautiful surroundings before we talk business!" He leaned towards the table's central screen which informed him of tonight's menu choices, including wines, with helpful illustrations of the various meal options. There were two more diners to join them; the sixth, as the screen informed them would not be attending.

When they had selected their choices from the screen, they sat back and waited for the drinks. Faure looked at Berenson. "How was your voyage here, Berenson? I had a smooth enough trip, for once — better than the last time, at least."

He grinned, nodding as a waiter showed him a bottle before pouring a sample. "I found a new sea-taxi. The sailor is a woman called Hooper, a change of career I gather from goods transport. Apparently, it is all getting too stressful in these harbours. She and her crew member had a narrow escape outside Dusseldorf when pirates struck all the freight vessels after using a bio-virus to lock down the port. They only managed to get away because the crew man had the presence of mind to dive under their boat and free them from a mine net, but he lost an arm in the process."

Both women grimaced. "He was lucky to survive," said Faure, nodding. "Water trade has become a risky business, particularly for those carrying bio-fuel. I suppose he'll have been given a new arm."

Berenson nodded. "As a matter of fact, he happens to be the son of a neighbour of mine. His arm is being cultivated right now and he is home for a month getting accustomed to a tech-arm while he waits for it. I gather he means to continue his career at sea once it is ready. He's a plucky lad and I'd have liked to have recruited him if he wasn't set on becoming freelance."

They were interrupted by the arrival of three fellow delegates to the table — a Chinese woman and two

American men. He knew both the Americans but not the young Chinese woman, who introduced herself as Lee and had taken the role over from a retiring member. As their drinks and food began to arrive, the talk turned to yields, newly developed species, pest control and security. Berenson felt weary and bored. Perhaps it *was* time for a career change, or at least a step up in the order. There was always the expansion challenge, although even that seemed too predictable, too easy. It would not be long now until the Conways capitulated and their outfit was under Greenergy's umbrella. They'd held out well, he'd had to admit, but the net was closing around them. It would only take a little more tightening to squeeze them into submission.

He speared the last chunk of rare steak and chewed, wrenched from his thoughts by a hand on his arm. Aceline. "What are you thinking, Berenson? You are not with us!" Her eyes creased, challenging.

He felt himself stir in response. "I was considering that out of the women at this table your company is the most desirable," he told her.

"What about the men?" she laughed, her voice low. He looked around. The other four were engaged in an earnest discussion about the benefits of marine fertilisers. The Chinese girl, Lee, could be no more than thirty and was keeping to a prudent minimum of contributions. Uzza, he thought opinionated and dominant. He studied her as she spoke to the American, Durant. Her hair was covered in a traditional scarf of the kind that many Arab women still wore, from devotion to culture more than an allegiance to any historic religion. Religion had largely died out in the world these days. But it also added to her air of mystique and he wondered if this was deliberate. The Americans were nodding but their faint smiles betrayed their dislike and distrust.

He regarded the French woman at his side. Their relationship, such as it was, relied on these conferences and was based on the conditions of opportunity and exclusivity. Though Aceline was married, her husband involved in the marketing side of the business, she was always able to overcome matrimonial loyalty on these company occasions. Berenson had never made a commitment to marriage, which he felt was an unnecessary and undesirable state. Spouses and children made life complicated. They meant obligations and emotions he could not afford. He was wedded to wealth, ambition and power — the very quality that attracted women to him in floods, even discounting his clean-cut, athletic build and striking features. He could take his pick, but preferred married women like Aceline who were committed elsewhere.

He shook his head at the offer of desert, wondering how soon he and Aceline would be able make their excuses and go to her suite. The evening's programme included a performance by a world class singer followed by dancing and an opportunity to meet with 'local guests'. 'Local guests' was a euphemism for the sex workers who would have been rented for the duration of the conference. The company spared no expense, shipping in prostitutes of every gender, body type and class to meet the desires and whims of its delegates. Berenson grimaced, wondering which of his fellow diners would be availing themselves of this facility; not the Chinese girl, he thought. She was too new. The Americans, he knew from past occasions, would throw themselves into the entire distasteful melee with gusto. And Uzza? She was an enigma. Who knew what her desires were?

What did Aceline make of her? They had fallen back in a post-coital languor on the huge bed in her suite. "Is she gay, do you think?"

She chuckled. "If a woman does not throw herself naked in front of you begging to suck your cock this does not always signify she is a lesbian, Berenson! No — I think Uzza is a woman with no interest in sex or in any kind of social interaction. People are not on her agenda except perhaps as commodities or obstacles. Did you notice her dinner choices? She ate only a little bread with some bean paste. And she does not drink. What motivates her, I don't know."

He frowned. What might be the desires and goals of a woman like that? What would she be doing now, at this moment? Not cavorting with a dusky 'local guest' of any colour or category, for sure, and not participating in any of the rowdy bar games that were prevalent at conference either. The Americans always harboured an enthusiasm for these activities.

He pushed the conjecture aside, turning instead to the sleek form of the woman beside him, sliding his hand between her legs where she remained damp from the last time. Her arms wound around his shoulders as she pulled him towards her.

Later, Aceline's breathing became regular as she succumbed to sleep, her breasts rising and falling, silhouetted in the console light, but Berenson, usually a sound, untroubled sleeper lay awake. The woman, Uzza, invaded his consciousness, her hard, glinting stare and unsmiling mouth, her preference for traditional attire and her cold, harsh voice. She'd been uninterested in the food or entertainment on offer. Why was she here?

After half an hour of fidgeting he got up and dressed, hearing Aceline's gentle snore continue as he let himself out of her room and walked back along the padded corridors and down until he regained the main lounge and bar areas, where drinking, carousing and groping was in full swing. He signalled a waiter, placed an order and sat to observe the scene, redolent of the lust portrayed in Dante's Inferno until he began to receive attention from both a beautiful black girl in a sparkling gown and a tall, slender boy wearing a designer suit. He waved them away, preferring to observe than participate.

Uzza sat at the desk in her suite, writing, using a pen and paper. She wrote with a quick, neat hand, stopping at intervals to lift her head and tap the pen against her teeth. After twenty minutes there was a soft knock at the door and she rose to open it, returning to her desk to insert the paper into an envelope as the visitor entered. His expensive shoes made no sound on the velvety carpet, his suit immaculate still, his blond hair tumbling across his face.

"Anything to report?" Uzza's expression remained impassive as she questioned him. "What is the man, Berenson, doing?"

The boy smiled, revealing his perfect, white teeth. "He has made an appearance in the salon but shows no interest in a sexual encounter. I think he has had a good session with the French woman, Faure. There is evidence of past liaisons during conferences. Your predecessor..."

"Yes. I have read all his intelligence. You can take this now and there will be a further one tomorrow. What of the Americans?"

The boy laughed. "They are involving themselves in the activities down there."

She studied him. "We need to know who the candidates will be, Ralph. Who is being groomed for government? See if you can pick anything up. I am mainly interested in the European sector but any other information is useful. Listen for news of mergers or take-overs."

He nodded, taking the envelope from her and sliding it into the inside pocket of his jacket and bending forward in a small bow before leaving as discreetly as he'd arrived.

Berenson was back in Aceline's suite in time for the breakfast she'd ordered. His wrist console messaged him that he must attend a meeting at ten. Across the table she placed her cup down and eyed him as he read.

"It's nothing — just a change of time for the dive today. Something to do with tides."

"Why silent? Is PAM not up yet?"

He shrugged. "Who knows? A malfunction, perhaps."

Longhope

The wind whipped along Longhope's alleys, gangways, landings and quays, sending plumes of spray over the walkways and ruffling the billows of seawater as they flopped on to the decking at the docksides.

Other than the relentless whistling wind and the slap of each wave on the sides of the jetty, the village was silent; soundless at midday, an unheard-of occurrence. The Submariner was devoid of customers, as was the provisions depot, the birthing centre and the community education rooms. A few remnants of placards were all that was left of the protesters. The corridors and stairwells of the re-loke buildings held no echo of trudging footsteps or children's shouts.

Early in the afternoon a pale vehicle approached from the hillside and pulled in by the pontoon warehouses to disgorge six figures, neon-suited, masked and bearing backpacks and weapons. They dispersed in pairs away from the front and into the apartment buildings, making a thorough sweep of each floor in an organised, practised routine: message, knock, shout. More figures arrived from the water, mooring with difficulty before clambering out to join the search.

Laura was in the tunnel office looking at yearly

returns when PAM announced a message. "Laura, Cath for you."

She froze the screen. The image that appeared was dark. Cath was not in her usual messaging position in her living room and her face loomed ashen from the surrounding gloom, hair in wispy strands framing it. She was struggling to speak. Laura sat up, eyes wide. "Cath! What's up? Where are you?"

Beads of sweat ran down the side of her sister's face. "Bedroom. In my bedroom. Listen." Laura felt her stomach churn.

"Sickness…"

"Are you sick? Oh God! What is it?" She saw her sister retch, where she lay on the bed, wiping the back of her hand across her mouth, groaning. "Cath — is anyone with you? Where is Spider?"

Cath lay back, listless, breathing laboured. "Gone."

"Gone? Where, Cath? Has he gone for help?" Her head made a slow turn to the side. "What then? Where has he gone?"

Her eyes opened, heavy. "Just… gone."

"He's left you? How could he do that? Has he taken Jack? Where is Jack?"

She raised herself up from the pillow, determined, eyes burning. "He's with our friends — with Maynard and Reuben. He'll be safe as long as they are." She fell back, exhausted.

Laura brought the screen news up, fumbling, feverish as she tried to reassure Cath. "We'll come down Cath. We'll come and get you. Stay put…"

"No!" The sick woman blurted before retching again. "You won't get past the cordon, Laura. It's lockdown."

And it was true. The screen was bearing breaking news, updated every thirty seconds; Longhope was in lockdown. First signs of disease had emerged late last night when crisis management had swung into operation. Nobody was to come into or out of the village unless authorised to do so. Drone footage revealed bio-suited police and medical workers looking like pale ants as they moved along the lanes and corridors of the village.

Cath wasn't finished. "One thing…" It was costing her a huge effort. "Do one thing for us."

Laura felt her heart thumping. "What is it?"

"Laura — take Jack. Safe… Keep him safe." She was spent now, falling back and mumbling, her consciousness fading.

Laura whimpered. "Cath — stay with me please! Please!" But the image clouded and broke up and she was gone.

Joshua was some distance away in a tunnel but made his way back to her when she messaged, holding her as she cried. The screen news continued to show updates. As yet there was no indication of the cause of the disease and foul play was not suspected. For the time being, contact with the inhabitants of the settlement would be restricted whilst rescue work was undertaken.

Laura twisted a hankie in her fingers. "What should we do?"

Joshua opened his hands. "We can't do anything for Cath. The medics are there in the village. You know how it goes. They quarantine anyone they think can survive and those who are not expected to are taken to rest."

She looked at him. "I promised Hugh! I promised I'd take her in…"

"Hugh didn't expect this, any more than we did. He would know we couldn't do anything right now. If they think she can survive they'll quarantine her and then we'll see. She can come and recuperate with us, perhaps, if they allow it."

"She's still my sister! I should have looked out for her. I've been selfish, Josh — and now look what's happened! It's my fault!"

He knelt by her and took her hands in his. "Laura, none of this is your fault. You cannot be to blame for a disease. We can't do anything right now except wait."

She hung her head. "She asked me if we can take Jack."

"Jack? What do you mean? Surely, he's with his father, isn't he?"

"No. He's gone. Spider. He's left them."

Her husband gaped in a gesture of incomprehension. "What kind of man leaves his child and partner in a disease-infested hell-hole and pisses off?" he shouted. She saw him set his shoulders in the square way that meant resolve. "All right. We'll go down for them. We'll fetch them back here."

"How? We can't get in there. And Cath is sick. Even if we got in, they'd never let us out with her. And we could get sick going there. We have a responsibility to Holly, and to Ethan, Kav and Ewa."

He frowned. "One of us has to stay. One of us needs to be here because of the running of this place. That should be you…"

"She's my sister!"

"Yes, but you know most about this place and can keep the farm going much more easily than I ever could. Christ knows what will happen to the business now. We won't be able to get down there to ship anything for the moment."

She lifted her head to protest and he cut in, stopping her. "There is a way we can do this safely. In those suits everyone looks the same. We have all the equipment we need here; bio-suits, masks and breathing gear."

"Josh you can't go down there on your own."

"No, I'm not proposing to. I'll take Ethan. No one has more experience of crisis conditions than he does, even at such a young age. He'll stay cool. I know he'll want to do it."

She bit her lip to stop it trembling. "I don't think I could stand to lose any more family members. And what would it do to Holly?"

"You won't lose anyone. We'll be safe in our suits. The worst that can happen is that we get rumbled and quarantined with all the others, in which case we'll get back eventually. You'll have to keep trying to message Cath and somehow we need to know where these friends are that are looking after the boy."

"Are you sure you want to take him, Josh? He is not part of our family."

"Ewa and Kav aren't related to us either, but we feel like they are. This Jack has been abandoned. Your sister is the nearest thing he has to a mother, as far as I can see. If she doesn't make it there'll be nobody but us."

"There are the friends who he's with at the moment."

"Laura, we don't know what state anyone is in. The friends might have cleared off, for all we know, or they might be sick — or dead!"

She nodded, fearful, but capitulating to his logic and turned back to the screen news. Numbers of the dead were as yet unconfirmed. The drone footage replayed as a reporter repeated the facts and described the scene. There were glimpses of workers below and once the appearance of two of them carrying a stretcher bearing a body bag. She shuddered. What if it were Cath?

Her husband returned with Ethan, the two laden with equipment. Ethan looked flushed, almost as if he was excited at what they were to do.

People had died in the tidy, sensible way they'd been told to, following the instructions the authorities provided. Once symptoms appeared, or they felt unwell, they were to stay indoors, rest in bed, drink fluids, mix with as few others as possible and leave their doors unlocked to enable access by health workers. Those who were well should not touch or share space with the sick, but should seek refuge with fellow healthy citizens.

They left the farm vehicle further back up the hillside amongst some bushes, where scouting drones could not spot it and crept down towards the dock, keeping to the sides of the track and once reaching the first streets and buildings darting from one doorway to the next as the small automated spies circulated overhead. They were still some way up from Cath's block when they noticed the first health and police workers entering the port administration offices. From here they decided to brave visibility and adopt a confident, authoritative stance, walking in a purposeful stride down towards the re-loke apartments.

Ethan gazed up at the grey tower blocks squatting on their concrete stilts, scaffolding companionways protruding at intervals to lead to external staircases. The access gangways were designed to be moved as the waters rose leaving lower stories submerged. How many residents were dead or dying inside the apartments? And was Cath one of them?

So far, they had not encountered one single living inhabitant of Longhope. The village had an eerie, abandoned feel, as if its entire population was on vacation. They rounded the corner of Cath's block. Two health workers were descending a stairway with a stretcher, prompting them to withdraw and try to gain entry from the other side. They would need to find Cath's flat first and assess her condition before attempting to find Jack. Ethan's heart thumped as they climbed the stairs towards the level that her apartment lay on. He would meet her. He would get to meet his mother. But would she be alive?

Hooper and Uzza

The forecasted storm had blown up overnight, prompting Hooper to seek shelter in a small bay which housed nothing larger than a few small boats used by locals as personal transport. She had often used this coast, with its towering cliffs and ragged inlets to wait out the worst storm surges but, since her abrupt change of occupation to carrier, she had rarely been obliged to hole up with a passenger. So far, the woman had eaten very little and spoken even less. While Hooper was accustomed to her own company for long periods and was delighted at her lack of demands, she felt uneasy. The current squall was forecast to go for several days, according to PAM, and the time could begin to hang heavy for her passenger.

On the whole the move to becoming a sea taxi was working out, although she missed some aspects of merchant seamanship. Ferrying human cargo required communication skills at a level beyond her capabilities to date, although she was working on them. She was not, had never been, one for the inconsequential chat some of her clients expected. And while Ethan had only been with her for a couple of years, she missed him too. He'd been her protégé, almost like a younger sibling and she'd felt a degree of pride in his development, knowing that she'd taught him all he knew. The ambush that caused his injury had all but devastated her and prompted her to re-evaluate her lifestyle. Sea taxi work, though still risky, held less potential for catastrophic events such as the capture of multiple vessels and consequent loss of life that carrying cargo retained.

Once there had been Futura, an extraordinary yacht that she'd loved like a child; swift, manoeuvrable and efficient, designed with Spartan accommodation and equipped with the most sophisticated technology. Now there was the ferry, Fulmar, which was a smaller 'cruiser', appointed for passenger comfort rather than 'real' work. She carried the requisite safety and communication aids plus items that Hooper considered essential for personal safety, the latest in scouting and weaponry technology but, other than these, she existed only as a means of transporting the very wealthy or important around the planet to their destinations.

The passenger cabin in the stern consisted of a slim bunk and shower. Hooper's own accommodation was little more than a shelf in a cupboard off the narrow galley. Meals and all other activities had to be undertaken in the mid-ship area which was furnished with a small, hinged table and a banquette. As skipper, Hooper spent much of her time on deck or observing the screen, vigilant and wary as a lifetime at sea had made her. This evening, as she leaned against the rail on the tiny forward deck, she heard the clang of the companionway as her mysterious passenger came up to join her.

The woman carried in her hand a small pair of eye glasses, a relic of a bygone age. She felt her way to the rail and raised her voice above the buffeting wind. "Do you mind?" she called. Hooper turned a rain spattered face to her, squinting into the gale and shrugged. The eye glasses were raised, the woman stumbling a little as the small boat bucked in the choppy waves.

Aware that it was not her job to pry into the travel purposes of her clients, Hooper was nevertheless curious about her companion. She had requested to travel north-east and to be set down as near as possible to The Wasteland. This was unprecedented. Few chose to travel to these uninhabitable regions, still less with the scarce amount of luggage this Farzul woman had. After scanning along the coastal strip with the eye glasses she shouted to Hooper above the gale. "Are you familiar with The Wasteland? What do you know of it?"

She led Farzul back down the steps and into the tiny dining area, where she threw off her jacket and sat at the screen.

"I haven't travelled extensively in the region," she began, "as you know, it is not deemed inhabitable. It is polluted beyond a level which is considered safe for life and which will not be safe in our lifetime or that of subsequent generations. There are no reliable predictions for when the pollution levels will drop down to a level considered safe to support human life. I haven't travelled far into the interior, merely dropped cargo at points along the coast." She brought up a map of the coast where Uzza had requested to be set down. "There is no infrastructure. No conventional ports or settlements. There are vestiges of previous docking facilities although they have fallen into disrepair and many are, of course, now submerged."

Uzza was studying the screen and following her words with a disconcerting intensity. She continued. "On the few occasions when I've had commissions there, I've minimised the time spent by acting with extreme speed and at the same time I've used a bio-suit and breathing apparatus for unloading and so on."

Her guest nodded. "And do you have this bio-apparatus on the vessel?"

Hooper paused. The woman could not be considering venturing into the interior? She would survive, at best, three days but the likelihood was much less. What could be her motive for such a foray? She ignored the question. "Although the Wastelands is considered uninhabitable, there are people living throughout the area. It is vast. Look." She indicated the map of The Wasteland. It began about a hundred miles from their current location and stretched across nearly one-third of the planet, encompassing hundreds of former countries and several seas. She showed Uzza another map illustrating population numbers and areas where people might be living.

"This is only speculative," she told her. "They are

thought to be nomadic, which is to say they…" Uzza wave her hand in a dismissive gesture.

"I know the meaning of nomadic. In times long ago, many of my ancestors were nomads. You have met some of these people? You must have, to have traded there."

Hooper turned from the screen to look at her. "I have seen some of them. I've dropped goods off to them. They are not like us. Most are very young, but don't look it. They are sick, many with disabilities, deformed limbs, blindness, skin lesions."

"What do you take there?"

"Medicines, sometimes protein substitute, tools."

"And how do they pay for these things? Do they trade?"

Hooper shook her head. "They have nothing to trade. In past ages there would have been valuable minerals and of course there were the fossil fuels the world depended on. Then there was the nuclear age and after that…"

Uzza broke in again. "Yes, yes, I am aware of the events. Thank you. Are you willing to provide the safety equipment for my disembarkation?"

Hooper frowned at the screen, thinking. "As your transport it is not my place to ask why you want to visit such a region. But I feel some responsibility as your carrier. Setting you down and leaving you there, even with bio-apparatus, will be handing you a death sentence. If the pollution doesn't kill you, the tribes

147

will."

"I can take care of myself, Hooper. You need not worry."

"Don't make the mistake of thinking that because the people are sick, they are helpless! They have years of experience of defending themselves against a hostile environment and a hostile world! They know me a little and they know why I come. You will be a stranger to them, with nothing to offer. They will not hesitate to kill you."

"How do they pay for the items you deliver?"

"They don't. Everything I take them is donated."

"By whom? Who gives the cargo?"

Hooper shook her head. "I can't tell you that." They fell silent for a few minutes.

"Maybe you should tell me why you want to go. Then we could plan better. You would need an exit strategy."

Uzza sighed. Her hands rested in her lap. There was, Hooper noticed, an unnatural stillness and composure in her and if she experienced a reaction to anything said, it was not evident in her body language. She lifted her head, seeming to come to a decision. "I go as an observer."

"An observer? Of what?"

"To make documentation…"

"You are an activist?"

"An activist? No, not as such. We seek only to know the truth."

"We? Who is 'we'? Is it an organisation?"

"To call us an organisation would be too formal a label. We are more a disorganisation, if you can understand. We share a conviction that nothing can, now, be changed, but we also share a desire to know and to record the events that are leading to the planet's inevitable destruction."

Hooper's chin set firm. "I don't believe it is inevitable."

Uzza inclined her head. "Why do you think this?"

"Since the struggles in the twenty-first century the world nations have implemented those strategies that were necessary to prevent dwindling resources and the deterioration of the world's climates into untenable conditions. Look what's been done! We no longer use the fossil fuels that were set to cause catastrophic weather events. We don't use aircraft, or make wasteful journeys like they did for tourism. We've got to grips with consumerism by reusing where possible. The rising of the seas is slowing. The world's population growth has stabilised. We don't war with each other now that oil is redundant…" her words dwindled and drifted off into a point over Uzza's head. She wore what passed for an indulgent smile, her hand raised to halt the skipper mid flow.

"Yes. Yes. So, we don't send poisonous gas into the air and we don't waste energy. But don't you realise that however much renewable energy, recycling and conservation we do now it makes no difference? The damage is done — *was* — done many years before you or I were born. In any case the weather is no longer the greatest threat to the planet, is it? We have the issues of disease control, piracy and a growing divide between the wealthy few and the masses to consider. There is another threat. Senate has agreed to lift the single child embargo. Why do you think this is? It is because the world's population is *dropping*. Disease has begun to impact on human numbers and there are many fewer children being born. Who are the wealthiest on the planet now, do you think?"

Hooper frowned. "Those who have not been affected by climate change; those who were lucky enough to be able to stay in their homes when the waters rose or were rich enough to be able to buy on high ground or purchase a floating home. Those who…"

Uzza was shaking her head. "They are the better off. They are not the very rich, the privileged. It is those who now stand in governance — they are the ones. It is in their interests to maintain the divide, to preserve their comfortable existence. And who are these new rulers of the world, do you think?"

Hooper looked puzzled. "I suppose they are people who've risen through the political system to become representatives for their nations and then their continents."

"Not any more. Their number is becoming dominated by power magnates. At the moment it is Greenergy and SOL who are increasing their places in

Senate but, as we speak, Zephyr is preparing to enter the political arena. Greenergy and SOL have plans for a merger. It is only a matter of time until all three become joined in one huge company. They will rule the world. This is no exaggeration, no fantasy. It is happening. These people have no interest in conservation and the endurance of the planet, only in the conservation of their own lives and lifestyles."

Hooper looked stung. She stared at the floor. "It doesn't have to mean the end of the world though, does it? We have to hope things will change for the better. No one can live without hope. I still believe earth can survive."

"It is your choice to believe what you wish. The facts speak for themselves. I may be able to change your mind. I am a fine judge of character, Hooper." She said this with no hint of pride. "I think your participation in our network would be an asset. You are able to travel freely and could be helpful in our communication network. We have to have people we trust. You are such a person, I think." Her face, impassive, gave nothing away. "Think about it, please. The world is changing rapidly and that change is accelerating. There may be little time left for any of us. You need not give me an answer now. But I will require collection from the point where we dock in two weeks' time. You should have reached a decision by then."

Hooper blinked. Uzza appeared to have decided for her. And she seemed in no doubt that the equipment she needed would be handed over without question. She excused herself and ascended the steps to the deck, more as a means of clearing her head than for any security purpose.

Hooper and Uzza

Two days later they were underway, making satisfactory progress in a breeze that was stiff but less of an impediment. Uzza had begun to spend more time on the small deck alongside the skipper, helping out with small chores or scanning the coast as they followed it along north and eastwards. Hooper had started describing how the shoreline had changed over the years. As a young sailor she'd caught glimpses of ice floes in the far north and frost on the land, sights never to be witnessed again.

"This is a lonely life," the passenger told her that evening as they sat at the small table to eat their meal. "What led you to choose it?"

Hooper stopped eating and gazed out at the dark sky. "My grandparents were from the former country of China and fled westwards when the conditions began to be unsustainable. The Chinese were always an adaptable people, able to make a life anywhere in the world. They fled to the Americas where they settled. My father was born there, studied hard and grew up to become a medic, specialising in disease control. When he and my mother met, he felt that European politics was more conducive to his work. He was ambitious for me, wanting me to do the same, placing a lot of pressure on me to pursue medicine as a career. I felt trapped." She paused and glanced at Uzza, who was studying her with rapt attention.

"As a child I never saw the real sea, only on screen or as a virtual tour. Travel restrictions had already begun to tether populations to their home towns and ours was in a central location, many, many miles from any coast. But I loved anything to do with boats and sailing. I used to construct toy vessels and experiment with propelling them and I fantasised about becoming free. By the time I was an adolescent I knew I wanted to go to sea, even before I'd seen the real thing for myself."

Her companion was nodding in encouragement. "And you had no ambitions for a home and a husband, for a child?"

The directness of the question was a surprise, coming as it did from this withdrawn, enigmatic woman. Hooper's brow wrinkled and she shook her head. "Not really. The single child rule had been in place for some time when I was born. I suppose we are a similar age, you and I? I was used to my own company, as I imagine you are." Uzza's face was impassive.

"My father didn't take it well. I tried persuasion, sulking and all the gambits offspring use to change their parents' minds. In the end I said I would leave to take up an apprenticeship either with or without his blessing, although without his backing it would have been almost impossible and he knew it. He agreed to a trial period and I didn't look back. Of course, they realised they'd lost me; that they would be unlikely to see me except in v-meets, but they came to accept it. My mother would have liked grandchildren, too. It *is* a solitary existence, mostly. I had a crew man for a while when I was trading but that is another story." She ground to a halt, feeling as if she'd rolled down a hill, having spoken more than she'd done in months.

"What about you?" she asked Uzza in an unrealistic expectation of reply. "No desire for a home and family life?"

Uzza closed her eyes for a moment and Hooper wondered if she was offended.

"It is natural for a woman to want a child," she began, "but the world is dying. It is not fair or moral or practical to introduce new life to this dying planet. Like you, I have made a conscious choice. There are few areas of our lives, in these times, that we have control over. In my work it is not sensible or realistic to form close relationships or to have anyone dependent on me. Encounters must be brief and relate only to the task we undertake."

After dinner Hooper went up on deck to check that the mast and rigging were secure and to scan the horizon and coast manually, a task which instrumentation had replaced but which she continued to undertake herself as a safety measure. When she returned, Uzza was again writing in a small book, an activity which fascinated the

155

mariner as she had seldom seen anyone using a pen and paper except in footage from history lessons as a child.

"Why do you write?" she asked her passenger. "When technology has replaced manual writing?"

Uzza finished the line she was writing and looked up. "Our ancestors would consider it a paradox, but paper has become the means of messaging that is most secret. Since communication became restricted to PAM, broadcast, v-meet and voice-technology, there is no other secure way to record data, observations and conversation. Think about it. Surveillance has increased beyond calculation in our lifetimes. Here at sea we can perhaps enjoy a relative degree of privacy where a signal may not reach but on inhabited land there is no such luxury. Life for most is lived under a scrutiny so ubiquitous it is akin to living under a microscope. Paper can only be seen by the person who has it. Paper can be destroyed."

"Where did you learn it?"

"I taught myself to write from watching history footage. It is not so difficult, although of course it is laborious in comparison to voice recording!" She bent her head to the notebook, signalling an end to the conversation and continued to make lines of marks on the paper with her pen.

In another day they were far enough north to need to make preparations for disembarkation. Hooper stood Fulmar out from the shore, far enough to be free of the poison zone but near enough to be able to get Uzza dressed and masked for her expedition. She would need to don the protective gear and wait outside while the yacht pulled in. Hooper explained how she would stand Fulmar as close as possible to the remains of the jetty using the small bio-motor, giving the woman as much of a chance as she could to step up on to it.

"But it has not been maintained," she advised her. "So you must be very careful to tread on the firmest parts. If you fall into the water it will be certain death and I cannot save you. The water will poison you in minutes, your skin, your lungs, your..."

"Yes, yes I realise, thank you." Uzza frowned in irritation, anxious to be getting on with her project. She had a small bag containing vials which she intended to use to collect samples. She peered out at the shoreline. "What is that, Hooper? Is a factory of some kind?" She pointed to an enormous structure consisting of once tall, grey chimneys, crumbling warehouses and the skeletal remains of high scaffolding.

"It is the ruins of an old fossil fuel processing plant," she told her. "They used to call them refineries. The oil would be piped from the wells across the land to the coast then prepared for use before being shipped on flat vessels they called tankers, which then used vast quantities of the fuel to transport it. It seems a nonsensical process to us now, but it was all they knew.

You must not remove your suit and mask for *anything.* You have your navigation aids?"

The woman nodded, waving her wrist.

"You will not be able to communicate with me regarding time or position. You must be here, at this exact spot in two weeks' time. I will bring Fulmar back to this position and remain here for forty-eight hours. If you have not reappeared by then I'm afraid I will have to assume the worst." She looked at Uzza. If she was afraid, she did not show it. She began to put on the suit, pulling it up and clipping the small bag on to the belt. In another bag there was a tiny water purification device and some nutrition packs.

"When I return," Hooper said, "I will be bringing supplies for them. There are a couple of cartons on the deck ready for you to sling up on to the quay when you land. They may not be visible to you but they will know you've arrived. The supplies should sweeten your arrival, I hope. If you're ready you can go on up now and we'll get on with it."

As the woman exited the tiny cabin and ascended the steps to the deck, Hooper gunned the small motor to bring them in towards the jetty. The rain had subsided into a fine drizzle and the waves to a rolling undulation. Fulmar's engine purred as she slowed and Hooper coaxed her to the protruding landing stage, trying to find a stable part for Uzza to clamber on to. There was a slight bump as they gained the side and she could see the cartons being lobbed across and Uzza making an agile spring up alongside them. While the area appeared to be deserted, Hooper knew there would be people watching. There was a different kind of surveillance here, in the Wastelands. The woman adjusted her belt, peered in at her and waved, before turning her back and setting off towards the shore and the towering ruins of the refinery.

She watched her go. The straight, resolute back unwavering as she drew further away until she was out of sight. She had to be admired. Hooper sighed and got Fulmar back into motion, away from the jetty and back towards safer waters. She set the small vessel's nose on a course south where she would be picking up two Zephyr executives from the Baltic coast and ferrying them to Dusseldorf. She felt glad to be on her own again after the stifling proximity of another being, the claustrophobia compounded by the woman's agenda. Uzza's overture regarding recruitment to her cause was lying heavy in her thoughts, interfering with her sleep and invading her concentration in a threatening manner.

After an hour she pulled on a spare suit as a precaution against lingering fumes and went outside to set the sails before returning to sit at the screen. She searched 'writing' and was soon absorbed in learning every detail about the activity. She rose only to rifle through a locker under the porthole from where she withdrew a small adhesive gun. She fetched a plate, clicked on the adhesive and began to make crude letter shapes.

Longhope

They waited in the shelter of the landing for a moment, listening and scanning up and below for white suits. Above the wind's keening whine there was another, insistent howl that was reminiscent, Josh thought, of the security dogs' baying, a chilling wail. His stomach contracted and he felt an acrid taste in his throat. He dipped his chin and squared his back, motioning Ethan to follow as he stepped out on to the narrow corridor that led along the apartments at this level. The howling grew louder as they progressed along the passageway. Ethan pulled at Joshua's sleeve and indicated some figures below on the pontoons. They pulled back against the wall for a moment, but the figures hurried on towards the warehouses, intent on their business. They inched further along, pausing outside of the door where the keening was loudest. Ethan jerked his head at the door, wanting them to investigate but Josh shook his in reply. They must get on with their task. Ethan stood his ground, rapping a gloved hand on the door and turning the handle, upon which the door opened and with no hesitation he stepped inside, giving his father no option but to follow.

Now, in the tiny lobby as the sound battered their

ears, they turned right into the compact living space and located the source. A woman on a sofa was rocking to and fro over a bundle on her lap, crying a shrill, persistent yowl. Her hair was a tangled mass, her eyes wide with despair. She was surrounded by a jumble of cloths and towels, stained and smeared with fluids that appeared to be vomit and blood. Ethan recoiled. The sight was repellent and he was in no doubt that the smell, if he were to shed his mask, would be intolerable. The woman had not seemed to notice their entry. Joshua stepped towards her, the movement catching her attention and she flinched, looking up at them and revealing the contents of the bundle she held. It was a child, dead; sightless eyes staring up, facial skin blanched and flecked. A small boy, no more six or seven years old, Josh judged.

She drew back as they approached, pulling the child in to her, eyes blazing in fury. "Get back!" she screamed. "Get out! Leave us alone!"

Josh held his hands up. "We mean you no harm. What is your child's name?"

She turned her face down to her son's lifeless form, cradling him and brushing strands of limp, blond hair from his forehead. "Lewis," she whispered. "He's my Lewis." Then her voice rose to a shriek. "You can't have him. You're not taking him! He's staying with me! Lewis!" The wailing resumed.

He stepped back. "I'm sorry. We won't take your boy. But some of our colleagues will be along in a minute to help you. OK?" He touched Ethan's arm and they padded from the room, closing the door behind them on the grieving woman and the dead boy. They paused in the lobby, using the spyhole in the door to check the corridor outside, then made as quiet an exit as they could and continued on until they reached Cath's apartment.

Here the woman's wailing had receded and no sound emanated from within. Wasting no time on knocking or calling, Josh opened the door. Ethan followed him into the porch. Beneath the bio-suit he was sweating and his stomach lurched in turmoil, hoping she'd be alive, wanting her to be here and not wanting her to be here and to have to face the reality of a meeting. There was still so much he wanted to know and was still so afraid to discover.

In contrast to the previous apartment, the small home was silent, devoid of movement and had an air of transience. The living room was neat and tidy but unadorned, yielding no signs of habitation; no personal effects, no digital frames, not a wall hanging, a rug or a throw. Apart from an unwashed cup in the sink and an overturned cereal box spilling on to the counter, there was nothing out of place in the minute galley kitchen. They moved through into the first bedroom, little more than a cupboard. It housed a narrow bed along one wall, a small desk under a screen and some storage drawers below a window. Unlike the rest of the apartment, the space was crammed with objects which, on closer inspection, revealed no obvious clues as to why they were there; a miniscule skull from some small creature, bits and pieces of machinery, remnants of packaging. There was a colourful quilt jumbled on the unmade bed, together with some unwashed items of clothing indicating that this was a young boy's room.

"This is the place." Josh spoke in a low voice, although restricted messaging meant that there was no danger of being overheard here in the apartment. Ethan nodded. "Do you want to stay here while I go and check out the main bedroom?" his father asked.

The young man shook his head and swallowed. "No, I'll come with you." Joshua placed a gloved hand on his arm then led the way out of Jack's room and in to the adjoining room; Cath's. He pushed the door. Again, it was tidy, except for the bed, which was wider than Jack's but still narrow. There was no window in here and the space surrounding the bed was confined to a strip only a very slim body would be able to access. Apart from this, there were two compact lockers stretching up to the ceiling and the ubiquitous wall screen.

The bedding was stained in a similar fashion to the previous apartment, although it seemed as if some attempt had been made to pull the covers over and make it tidy. But the room was empty of people.

They backed out. "We need to move on, Ethan", Josh urged, as Ethan paused to stare at the space. "Ethan! Now!" Josh barked, receiving a nod in return.

Back in the hallway they stopped, hearing voices passing outside and footsteps. They held their breath, silent until the steps receded and they caught the faint clanging as feet descended the stairs. Ethan opened the door a cautious sliver and they walked out, along and up a flight to the next landing to locate number twenty-five, Maynard and Reuben's apartment.

Their door stood out, having been painted an unauthorised emerald green and bore a handcrafted sign carved with the symbol of two hands pressed together: Namaste, the old sign of greeting in a long-forgotten religion. They followed the routine of knocking gently before trying the door and found themselves in an Aladdin's Cave of a hallway, studded with objects and decorations in a riot of colours. Josh called out, low voiced as they moved on. "Hello?" They walked into a living room identical in size and shape to the previous two but as different as a palace to a laboratory, decked in handmade art, colourful throws and pieces of sculpture fabricated from recycled objects. Ethan stayed to gaze around the room and his father moved out into the packed kitchen where, despite the plethora of equipment, everything was clean and in order. He came back in. "Nobody in there."

The bedroom doors were closed. Pausing outside the larger room they listened. There was a sound of breathing, rattling and laboured. Someone was in there but in a poor condition. Josh knocked softly before turning the handle and opening. Again, the small space was full of colour and soft furnishings, the small double bed draped with patchwork and embroidery, but upon it lay the obese form of a man, propped by pillows but sweating and struggling for breath. He lifted one hand as they approached.

"Maynard?" Josh whispered.

He dipped his head in affirmation. "Joshua?" he managed to wheeze.

Josh nodded. "Yes, Josh and Ethan. We've come for..."

May lifted his hand again and gestured towards the doorway. "Bedroom," he gasped.

Josh turned to Ethan. "Check out the small bedroom," he murmured. "The rescue workers are on their way," he told the sick man. "They'll see you're all right." He paused. "Thanks for looking after the boy... and good luck!"

The enormous man raised his wet, pink face to Josh and gathered himself for the effort of speaking. "Take care of him," he breathed; and there were tears mingling with the perspiration on his cheeks then his chin dropped back on to his chest and he was spent.

Joshua pulled the door shut before joining Ethan, who'd opened the door to the smaller room and found a child sitting in silence on the carpeted floor in one corner, hugging his knees up under his chin as if to make himself invisible. Ethan appeared to be frozen to the spot. Josh dropped down on his haunches in front of the boy. "Hello... Jack, isn't it?" Jack's face rotated so that one cheek was pressed against the wall, trying to shrivel his body further back and disappear. "It's OK," Josh continued. "We've come to fetch you. You'll be safe with us. We live on a food farm. There's no disease up there on the hillside. Do you have any belongings with you?" The boy shrank back still further.

"I'm not going nowhere," he mumbled.

"Has your friend Maynard been looking out for you, Jack? I know he is your friend, but he's sick now. If you stay you might get sick too. I am Joshua and this is Ethan. Your friend told you we were coming, didn't he? Cath and your Dad…"

The boy faced him, eyes glaring. "They're coming back for me! I'm waiting here for them! They're finding somewhere safe and then they're coming to fetch me. You can get lost!"

Ethan pointed at his wrist console. The time was ticking on. The longer they spent here the more likely it was that they'd be discovered as imposters and not the official rescue party of health workers. Josh thought and then began again. "OK, Jack, here's what we'll do. You can come back with us tonight and get something to eat and stay over at the farm. Then we'll bring you back tomorrow with some supplies, if you like. The only thing is, your friend Maynard won't be here then because the health crew will find him soon and take him to quarantine to make him better. That's what'll happen to you, too if you stay!" He sat back on his heels to gauge the effect of his words. The child stared at him then reached out for a small rucksack which he gathered to him before unfolding his limbs and standing. In spite of his bulky jacket it was clear that he was underweight from the stick thin wrists that protruded from his sleeves and the gaunt angles of his face. Joshua let out a quiet breath and motioned the boy to go ahead of him so that he was sandwiched between them as they left the apartment.

They were halfway down the second staircase when they encountered the health workers coming up.

"Hi. Any more live ones up here?" A woman's voice quizzed them. Ethan gestured back up the steps. "We found two, but they are in no condition to walk. They'll need transporting. We'll take this one down if you go back for some stretchers. But you'll need to take a look first. One's in very bad shape." He put every particle of authority he could muster into this command, while praying they didn't notice their lack of official logo on the suits.

They walked back along the corridor and down the staircase, listening all the while and scanning the area beneath the apartment block. Once they'd gained the gangway, they made for the solid ground higher up the village, keeping to the sides of the buildings and taking care to look purposeful. They were almost on the lane that led to the farm when they heard shouts and turning, saw a group of suited workers further back by the apartments waving and calling them. They were being beckoned back to the village and the rescue vehicles.

Ethan thought fast then gave a vigorous wave before pointing up towards where they'd left the farm vehicle. With luck they would assume they had official transport up there.

"Let's pick up the pace," Joshua urged. "But whatever you do, don't run!"

The boy seemed as anxious as they were to avoid the authorities and they strode briskly to the bend, where Ethan risked a quick look back over his shoulder and saw that two workers had broken away and were trotting in their direction. "Let's run!" he hissed and now that they were out of the workers' sight all three scurried up the track until there was enough cover at the side, diving into the tangled undergrowth; Jack nimble and swift, the two men slower, encumbered by the suits. They made their way along and up using the mesh of weeds and bushes for cover until at last the farm van was in sight and without pausing to check if they were still being followed, they wrenched open the doors and leapt inside. Joshua started it up, wrenching the wheel as the van skidded into life and wound its way up in a spray of stony earth.

He spoke over his shoulder to Jack as he drove. "Well done Jack! Just so you are prepared, when we get to the farm, we'll need to run a couple of checks on you so we're going to use one of our polytunnels and take you in while we do them. Is that OK with you? We need to know that you're free of disease before we take you to the house."

He took the boy's silence as compliance, although he had no plan for the possibility that the child was sick. If he was, they would have to find a way to deal with it.

After five minutes of checking the track behind them, Ethan concluded they were not being followed and they wound their way up to the farm.

Earthsend

She could tell he'd arrived from the sounds; the crunching feet and murmurs outside, the opening of the door and the hearty exclamations of welcome. But she remained seated at her table in the window alcove, staring at the drops as they wove their way down the pane, joining forces to run faster as they neared amalgamation on the sill. She waited until she heard her father's tread on the stairs, knowing he would come, hearing his knock before he entered and walked across to sit on her bed.

"Are you coming down soon?"

She nodded, still facing out.

"We can't do this without you, Holly. You know how I rely on you at the tunnels? Well this is the same. We need you on the team, more than we ever have! We've lost two people we loved more than anything in the world. But this boy, Jack, he's on his own without anyone now, except for us."

Her eyes were wide when she faced him. "Why? Why's he come? I don't get it. If his dad had to leave, why didn't he go too?"

"It's too dangerous for him. Cath and his dad, Spider that is, they've had to disappear. The police think he's had something to do with all the break-ins; or at least have organised some of them. He may not have been the one to carry them out."

She nodded slowly. "Why has she gone then, Cath? She's his mum. She should be looking after him, not us."

Josh rose, walked over to her chair and placed a hand on her shoulder. "Holly, Cath isn't Jack's mum. She's looked after him like he was her son, but he isn't hers. He's Spider's son. His mother disappeared when he was three years old. Cath's the nearest thing he's had to a mother. We've had a tough time here but he's had much worse, worse than anything we can imagine."

She frowned at her father. "So Cath, she never — she doesn't have any children?"

He gazed down at her for a moment then took his hand away, decisive. "Come with me, Holly. Come down. I need to show you something."

She followed Joshua downstairs and along the flagstone passage into the annexe — Hugh's quarters, untouched since he left except for Ewa and Kav's brief occupation. They crossed to his precious bookshelves, the collection he'd loved and conserved only to leave behind when he went. Josh perused the shelves, scanning along until he found the old photo-book, withdrawing it with care, an ancient, hard-backed book containing real, paper photographs.

They sat together on Hugh's comfortable, squashy old sofa. There were pictures of Hugh and Ellen's wedding, of them emerging from an historic building into a crowd of smiling, waving people. "That was the chapel, Holly. In those days most people got married in a real building. And look, here is Ellen, your grandma, with Cath as a baby and then there is one of your mother, too. Your granddad went on printing real photos on paper long after everyone else gave up and went to screen. Here are Cath and your mum together as little girls."

Holly's fingers reached out to trace the small rectangle of shiny paper. She was silent. Josh turned the page, slow and measured. The little girls became older, playing in the garden, climbing up a ladder into a tree house that skirted a sturdy tree. Holly gasped. "That's our apple tree!"

Her father laughed. "Yes, you've seen the remains of their tree house. It's amazing how it hangs on there, clinging to the tree in all the gales."

"And the sun is shining!"

"Yes, there were still a few sunny days then." He turned the page again. The girls became teenagers, showing off, dressed for special occasions. Then on the next page there was a photo of Ellen with another new baby on her lap.

Holly stared, puzzled, then tilted her head. "Did Grandma have another baby? Who is she?" She lowered her voice to a whisper. "Was the baby taken to rest?"

He shook his head. "No, Ellen didn't have any more babies. This one was not hers. It was Cath's." Holly

172

looked confused.

"It isn't Jack?"

"No. As I said, Jack isn't Cath's child, but she did have a child, a son. The baby is Ethan. Ethan is Cath's son. He's your cousin, not your brother."

Holly gaped at the picture. It was a giant leap to understanding. Ethan was not her brother, but her cousin. She shook her head. "But why, why did Mum end up caring for him? How come she was allowed to? What about the single child policy? He'd have been taken away and given to a childless couple! Why wasn't he?" Josh sighed. He was finding the revelation as hard to impart as Holly was to grasp.

"Your granddad Hugh and Ellen started off looking after Ethan and they pretended he was theirs because nobody wanted him to be taken away and rehomed with a childless couple, but after a while Ellen started to become forgetful so your mum and I took him on, even before we were married. And he was fifteen before you came along — almost grown up. We got away with caring for him for two years before he went to sea. We were lucky. And when you came along, we thought we were the luckiest people alive!"

Joshua swallowed as he glanced down at his daughter. She was having to grow up too quickly and take on a burden too heavy for childhood to bear.

They sat for a long time looking through the photo-book. "Now you know where to look," Josh told her, "You can come and see the photographs whenever you want. I know you'll take care of them."

She closed the old book with great care as if it might wither to ashes in her hands, stood and carried it back to the shelf. "I'm ready now, Dad. Let's go and meet him."

The boy sat hunched at the kitchen table, hands in his pockets, parka still dripping to the floor from where it was draped on the back of his chair. Holly pulled out the chair opposite him and sat with her hands resting on the table top. "Hello Jack. I'm Holly. Do you remember me from school?"

"I know." The words came out fast and bitten off with little lip movement. He had a thin, sallow face topped with lank, dark hair. She could see the tips of his ears protruding. She leant forward. "I can show you the farm, if you like. We can go now if you want, before dinner."

He shrugged but stayed put.

"Or we could just look around the house tonight and have a longer tour tomorrow? And see the tunnels!"

There was a lengthy pause before he spoke. "Where do I sleep?"

Josh stirred. "I'll take you up, Jack, and show you your room. Follow me." He bent to pick up the rucksack but the boy snatched it up, cradling it in his arms like a baby then followed Josh upstairs, where he stayed, even when first Laura messaged him then Holly crept up and knocked at his door to tell him dinner was ready.

"He'll be hungry." Laura frowned as she placed a

dish on the table. Her husband distributed plates and cutlery.

"He'll come down and eat when he's hungry enough."

In the morning there was no sign of Jack except that bread, milk and an apple had been taken from the kitchen. Laura peered out at the low, drizzly mist. His parka coat was absent from its hook in the porch.

"Holly, I need your help."

Jenny Philips's image drifted into the room, her kindly smile and plain, open face a reassuring presence. But she looked thin and gaunt, and older by many years. Holly could see that her teacher was still in the quarantine facility from the white walls and the machinery in the background. Holly sighed. How come everyone needed her help? She could do with help herself.

"I know you're having a hard time at the moment," her teacher continued. "You've lost two people who meant a great deal to you. But you know I've come to rely on you quite a bit this year, you and Nell. There is something I need you to do now. You can say no, but please hear me out first."

The girl's attention was caught, perhaps for the first time since Hugh went. She frowned at the teacher but there was a light of curiosity in her eyes. What could she, Holly, a ten-year-old girl do to help Mrs Philips?

Encouraged by the lack of rebuff, Jenny resumed. "I've been worried about Jack ever since he started at

175

our school. He hasn't checked in very often and he's missed most of his assignments. Now he is staying with you perhaps you could try to get him interested." She paused. Holly had become disinterested herself these last few weeks. She was like an empty shell that had once housed an enthusiastic, motivated intelligence. Jenny needed to get her back on track. These two troubled children might be able to help each other.

Holly gazed at her teacher's round, ruddy face. "I can try," she said. "The thing is I don't know him at all. I don't know what he likes or…"

"I know one thing, Holly. You are very, very good at helping others and making them feel special. That's why I'm asking you."

"OK. I will try. I'll do my best. It's what my granddad would have wanted."

Jenny Philips let out the breath she'd been holding. "That's the spirit!" She wished, as always, that she could take the girl in her arms and hug her. It was the last assignment that Jenny Philips was to make in her career. She succumbed to complications while still in the quarantine unit and never made it back to Longhope and her beloved, virtual classroom.

Holly donned her rainwear and let herself out of the back door into the garden. Since her grandfather had gone, with no one to tend it, the space had begun to look unkempt. Clumps of yellow rape plants had sprung up, invading the rose beds and the vegetable plots and obliterating the paths. She made her way to the apple tree, where the branches and the few scraps of timber that had once been the tree house offered a degree of shelter, rested her cheek against the rough, knobbly bark and looked up into the canopy. Most of the old tree's leaves clung on whatever the onslaught of wind and rain, the branches bending under each assault but staying attached. She pulled her hood up, stepped away and made her way around the side of the farmhouse to begin searching for Jack.

Earthsend

Ethan was having to make a number of adjustments. It was as well, Laura said, that he was young and strong. He'd suffered more trauma than most people undergo in a lifetime and he was not yet twenty. Since going to sea he'd changed physically and emotionally, even before the injury. Now he'd learned to use the tech-arm while his new limb grew in the laboratory, but the attempt to accustom himself to farm life was proving trickier than any adaption to loss of a body part.

Laura had warned him to tread softly in his re-acquaintance with Holly. "She knows you are not her brother," she told him, "but she is still in shock from Farlow's death and the leaving of your grandfather." In the moments they were together he'd told his cousin about his voyages, the lands he had visited and the life at sea. He'd also asked her to help him to learn about food production, a strategy to build her confidence rather than educate him on the subject. Nothing made her more proud, than sharing her extensive knowledge of plants and cultivation.

They shared more than they knew; Josh and Laura were parents to both of them and they both grieved over the loss of Hugh and of their grandmother Ellen before him. When she'd become more comfortable with Ethan, Holly was able to ask him what she'd wanted to know since the accident; what his tech-arm felt like. He'd smiled, only glad that she'd asked. "It feels kind of heavy," he replied. "Even though the material it's made from is lighter than flesh and bone. It's like having to lift objects with your shoulder, but it's getting easier all the time. I kind of like it now and I might end up wishing I'd kept it instead of the grown arm. I can do anything with it now!" And she'd noticed. Not only had Ethan shown a religious fervour in his devotions to the exercises he'd been given but he threw himself into farm work with gusto, aware that they were short-handed and of the difficulties that Laura and Josh faced over security and challenging weather conditions.

One morning after he'd returned from his assignment with Hugh, as he and Laura worked in one of the tunnels installing wires to support the new espalier apple trees, she asked him if he'd ever v-met his mother. He'd been silent for some minutes, grappling with the fixing of a wire on to a hook, clumsy with his mechanical fingers. She'd had to refrain from helping, knowing he must overcome such hurdles unaided.

"She sent me a lot of meet requests," he said, his back to Laura while he tried the tie again. "I mean, I never knew what to say to her. I didn't know her as my mother or anything."

"Did you know your grandfather wanted her back

under our roof, Ethan? How would you have felt about that?"

He paused, facing the slender sapling. "I don't know. I wouldn't have wanted her to start being a mother to me! It would have been weird; but if it was what everyone else wanted... Did you want it?" He turned to face her; the wire now fixed in place. His face was flushed.

She stared at him. "I don't know. I don't know either." Had it been selfish not to want Cath here? She sighed. Nothing about their lives was impervious to change, not their livelihood, their dwelling, their family or the weather.

Ethan moved along to the next small tree, becoming more adept with the use of his mechanical fingers as he gripped the wire. The fine motor control was developing. He was speaking again as he worked to secure the tree's limbs. "In any case, once I've got my new arm, I'll be returning to the water full-time."

Laura bit her lip. She was working in parallel on the opposite side of the tunnel. "We thought perhaps you might stay on now; have a change of direction, now we no longer have Farlow."

"I'm not a farmer, Laura, and I never will be. I want to get back to sea. I need to. And now you have Jack, he'll be able to help, won't he, once he's got used to things."

Laura grimaced. Jack's arrival into the household had not been easy. He behaved like a wounded animal, skulking and suspicious; spending long periods of time in his room or out of the house, she knew not where and rarely eating meals with the rest of them. He preferred to creep out from his lair during the night to forage in the kitchen and to disappear during the day. As yet he showed few signs of becoming integrated into their family or into farm life, and no interest at all into the workings of the enterprise. It was Ethan she needed to keep at home, where she knew he was safe.

"Even after…"

"Yes! Even after losing my arm. I've thought about it all the time. The world is no safer on the land than it is at sea. Look what happened to Farlow and to Cath! And I can make a difference out there on the water. I can't allow this…" he jerked his head towards the tech-arm, "to obliterate all my skills and experience. I'm going back to Futura. So, it would have made no difference if Cath had come or not. I won't be here."

Later, after dinner, he excused himself. "Why don't you stay and watch the game with us?" Laura asked him. They had reserved a showing of the Europe versus America cup final, feeling that they all needed to lose themselves in an escapist activity. But he declined.

"It's OK. I have a few things to do."

Josh and Holly exchanged knowing looks as he left the table. Laura stared from one to the other. "What?" she asked them. "What do you know that I don't?"

"You really haven't noticed?" Joshua sat back and smirked at her. "You haven't seen the way he looks at her — looks at them both?"

She frowned. Holly intervened. "He's visiting Ewa, Mum. He helps out with Kav. He likes them a lot, I think..." she tailed off, reddening. Laura's mouth dropped open, making them both laugh — a welcome sound.

"Then he may change his mind about leaving, do you think?"

Josh smiled. "It's early days, love. Let's wait, give them a chance and see what happens."

"I'd like him to stay. He is still a brother to me and always will be. I don't care who his mum and dad were." Holly felt that nothing could be better than three of her favourite people coming together and living on the farm. She missed Hugh and wanted to keep everyone she loved around her.

Kav was fussing. His mother stood at the window in Hugh's sitting room rocking him and humming. Ethan crossed to her. "Shall I take him for a bit? You can relax, get a shower or something — if you want?"

Since Hugh left, Ewa had stayed in his quarters with Kav. Though she retained a solemnity, a quietness that wasn't there before, her face was starting to regain its natural, rosy glow, most evident when she was attending to baby Kav. He was her consolation in those early weeks after his father died; the reason for her to get up each morning, to survive each day, to be alive.

Then Ethan was there, a quiet, solid presence. Hurt too, but strong and resilient. He took care of the small things: Kav's laundry, clearing out the ashes and laying a new fire, bringing in logs and remaking it, bringing her drinks while she fed her infant son. He asked nothing of her and she grew to trust and rely on him. After a time, they began to talk; he of his fears and hopes and his plan to return to sea once his arm was ready and replaced, she only of Kav and his future. What he'd done that was new, a smile or a sound he'd made and what she hoped for him.

So, they drew together, unnoticed at first by the rest of the family, or so they thought.

Holly and Jack

Jack was leading Holly along the border between Earthsend and Greenergy Longhope. They were sidestepping along the tall conifers, Holly flattening herself into the trees as she went, as the boy had shown her. She'd no idea yet why they must avoid being seen.

"I've been over there, hundreds of times!" she told him. "It's no problem! The boss there, Berenson, knows us all very well. We go there at Christmas sometimes and he has a sort of party and gives us nice food."

Jack turned and shushed her, pointing up to where a drone hovered. "They can see *and* hear us," he whispered, then dropped to his haunches, signalling her to do the same. He wanted to show her something, he said, despite her protests that there was nothing she didn't know about Greenergy.

Holly was discovering surprising things about Jack. When he finally acquiesced to being taken on a 'tour' of the farm he'd been unimpressed by the seemingly limitless tunnels, exclaiming most over the bio-vehicles, which he'd demanded immediate access to and been disappointed at her response. He showed no interest in the inhabitants of the tubes — the fruit and vegetables, except to request a banana or an orange, and was disgruntled by having to suit up and use the scrub bath before he could enter.

But he knew his way around. He knew how to get to the tunnels and the location of Farlow and Ewa's house. He knew where all the tracks went and how to move around the property unnoticed.

"You've been here before!" she blurted one morning when, whilst showing him around the farm outhouses, he'd unlatched the door to the fuel store.

"A few times," he'd replied over his shoulder as he opened the hatches to some hoppers and peered inside.

"When? When have you been here? No one's allowed to. You're not supposed to travel."

He shrugged. "There's no one to stop you. I go where I want. You don't have to tell anybody where you are. Well *I* don't."

Now they were on their way to Greenergy, unseen. "There's no way into Greenergy except by the front gates," she'd assured him, "and by invitation. And there's nothing much to look at either. It's just a farm, much bigger than ours and not so interesting, because they only grow one crop. But there's the factory part where they press the plants for the oil. I've seen it all already."

His superior smirk said it all. He pushed the lank hair back from his face. "There are plenty of ways in. I can show you."

"How do you know?"

"People come up here all the time."

"To steal, you mean?"

He nodded. "Some, yeah, but not all of them. There are others who come to watch."

She frowned. "Your dad, Spider, is he one of those?"

He remained silent.

"Is he?" she pressed him.

He lifted his chin a little higher. "My Dad's a legend," was all he said.

"Where is he, Jack? Do you know?"

"No, I don't, but I know he'll come back for me. He always does. He'll be away working for the Organisation somewhere. When I'm older I'm going to do the same."

"The Organisation? What is that?" But if he heard her, he gave no sign and continued leading her, his straggly mop of hair and pale neck facing resolutely to the front.

They walked along the perimeter fence for a few minutes until they came to a part where several buildings were incorporated into the boundary. One wall protruded a half a metre in front of another, where a new wall began. Jack grinned at her before placing a hand high up in a slight indentation and hoisting himself up, his lower foot finding a small crease where some mortar had dropped out. He moved his spare hand up towards the top where a corrugated roof protruded and heaved his frame up, diving forwards on to the sloping panel, showering Holly with detritus from the runnels in the corrugation as he went. Then he swivelled around and hung, grinning from his elevated position, beckoning her up.

She screwed her face up at him, but searched for the holds and pushed up, grabbing at his dangling hand and feeling herself hauled up until she was belly forward on the roof, alongside him, peering over the Greenergy compound from a viewpoint she did not recognise. She tapped his shoulder. "What about the *drones*?" she mouthed, pointing to where one hovered in disconcerting proximity. But he shook his head and whispered, mouth to her ear.

"They don't circulate this far. Look, they are on a loop over the tunnels." And it was true. The surveillance machines served to secure the safety of the crop from overhead. Here, where they were overlooking Berenson's private apartments, a roving camera was considered sufficient.

Jack was whispering again. "Your friend hasn't been here for a quite a while. His big car hasn't been in the garage and he hasn't been in or out of the house."

"He's not my friend! We don't have anything to do with him now. My Dad blames him for what happened to Farlow. Berenson recommended the dogs. And he would like the farm to belong to Greenergy. They've taken thousands of food farms. Dad says it won't be long before they own everything."

"Well you have to wonder. They don't use dogs here, do they?"

"No but they are rich! They can afford all the technology because the company pays for it."

They fell silent, watching the courtyard, the surveillance drones circling in a slow, monotonous loop. Jack touched her arm. He turned his face to hers. "Stay low!" he mouthed. A door opened in what appeared to be a warehouse or a machine store and a dark, thick-set man emerged carrying a bucket. He crossed the yard and disappeared around the corner of the dwelling. Jack hissed at her. "There's that man. You'll know him. He worked at your place for a while."

She frowned. "I've never seen him. Who is he?"

"It's that dog-handler, the one who was working for your dad."

Holly's stomach lurched. She'd never seen the dog-handler, lodged in a small hut within the corridor of fencing that surrounded their property, having been warned by her father not to approach the animals or their supervisor. "What's he doing here?"

The boy shrugged. "He works here, for Greenergy, I think. Didn't you see him when he was at your place?"

Holly bit her lip. "No. I wasn't allowed anywhere near him or the dogs. But I didn't know he was here, working for Berenson."

They were silent for a moment. "He could have stopped them," Jack murmured.

"What do you mean?"

"He could have stopped the dogs attacking that man who worked for your Dad. Farlow — wasn't that his name? Why do you think he didn't?" He looked at her, mere guileless curiosity in the wide set of his features.

"How could he stop them?" Holly's pulse was racing and she felt sick.

"Well that man," he jerked his head in the direction the dog handler had gone, "he's the handler, so he has to control the animals. And you know how he does it, don't you?"

She shook her head, concentrating.

"They are just as likely to go for him as for anyone else, so when they're born, they have a little microchip implanted in their neck and when he needs to stop them doing something he doesn't want, he just presses a button on his control panel. The button gives them an electric shock then they drop to the ground. He could have pressed the button that night. Why do you think he didn't?"

Holly rested her chin on her hands, staring at the space where the handler had been. "How do you know all this stuff? How do you know who that man is?"

"My Dad knows him. He's called Porc; at least that's what Dad calls him. He's been round to our place a few times."

Holly's voice rose. "We need to get back. We need to tell my parents about this. This man, Porc, he is a murderer!"

"Shh! Keep your voice down! We'll talk about it on the way back, but there's nothing your parents can do about it, is there? The bloke is dead. You can't bring him back."

They slid down in a surreptitious wriggle and dropped back down on to the earthy fringe by the wall then keeping low, crept back to the trees.

After a few minutes a bleeper alert sounded, followed by the clanging of an automatic door beginning to elevate and a low, sleek car glided into the yard. A woman stepped out of the car; tall, thin, angular and dark-skinned. She wore ethnic headwear and carried a slim, black case. She walked swiftly to the house and spoke into her console, upon which the door opened and she stepped inside.

Hugh

He'd been dreaming about the farm. The images had been vivid enough to convince him he was there, the sensation continuing as he woke. He'd been there, walking along the tunnels with Holly, explaining something, needing to tell her something urgent but the words seemed locked inside him. Try as he did, they remained thrust down. He knew he'd been opening his lips to say them, to shout them, but no sound would emerge. He woke to the darkness of the room, broken as always by dazzling swords of light scything through the narrow window slits and a flickering, a shadowy figure interrupting the shafts by moving across them. As he became conscious, a heavy cloud of grief and longing settled back over him.

The figure became visible, standing in front of him, swathed in bulky, flowing robes. It was Sulima or Fatima, or perhaps Abdul, he didn't know. Lately he'd been unable to distinguish between any of them. Something was being offered to him; a hand, open, proffering tablets. He took them. Another hand urged water with which to swill them down. He complied in obedient silence, swallowing in noisy gulps until the water was gone then leaning his head back against the chair and closing his eyes as if the mere effort of taking pills had exhausted him. For a moment he wondered why he'd ever considered it a fine idea to come here, to the sun, to sacrifice everything he held dear, everything he loved, all he could have had for a little longer if he'd have chosen to stay.

In his clear-headed moments he realised his family must never know and this was the reason his messaging had become less frequent. He could no longer remember the last time he'd worked in the gardens or walked and talked with Ahmed. The groups of children who came to help out and learn had long since ceased to visit. He couldn't recall the last time he'd stepped outside, either into the searing white heat of the day or the clear, star-studded night.

After a few minutes he was aware that someone was talking to him, someone sitting next to him, leaning towards him and speaking in a soft, insistent tone. He struggled to sit up straighter in the chair and turned towards the voice, recognising the owner of it as Ahmed, the man he'd thought of as his friend and confidant but realised now was just a handler of goods; the employee who managed the elders.

"Are you ready, Hugh?" he was asking. Hugh frowned, looking down at his lap, struggling to think. What must he be ready for?

"Have you forgotten, my old friend? We are taking you all on an excursion today! You are to meet up with your friends from the bus." The voice was disarming as ever. Hugh looked up and gazed at the man's eyes, clear, steady, determined and at odds with his mouth, which wore a patient smile. The old man summoned a resolve and sat straighter, ignoring the smiling mouth.

"I am ready," he replied, doing his utmost to suppress the querulous note he knew must be evident. As he rose to his feet, Ahmed offered a firm hand and placed a blanket around his shoulders. "You will not need anything," he assured him. "Everything will be provided."

As he stepped out from the squat, white dwelling that had been his home for such a brief period Hugh paused to glance back. The woman, Sulima as he now saw, was sweeping out the entrance, filling him with the curious sensation that it was he, himself, was being swept out of the place. Ahmed's hand pressed his elbow, guiding him towards the bus and the driver who'd brought them leant down to help pull him up the steps. At the top he stopped to scrutinise his fellow passengers, seeing those same elders he'd arrived with; but how they had altered! There was no intrigued gazing from the windows, no sense of anticipation or happy contemplation of the pleasures to come. This time their eyes were dulled in recognition of defeat, of anticlimax, the acknowledgement of their own poor judgement. All stared down or at the seat in front or had closed their eyes. All were silent. Hugh felt himself nod. Yes, he was empty as they were. He shuffled wearily down the aisle until he found a seat and sank down into it.

It was dark when he woke again, the only light emanating from the bus lights, which illuminated a wedge of stony track, bluish under the night sky. They were far out in the desert now. Hugh had no idea where, although like the others he'd guessed it didn't matter, from the euphemistic use of 'excursion' and the assurance that he would need nothing.

When the vehicle pulled up, he rose, pulling himself out of the seat and joined the queue making their way along the bus and down the steps, helping each other and assembling in a ragged group outside in the cool air, clutching the flasks of water and the packets they'd been given as they stepped out. There were coughs and involuntary groans as they drew together, pulling their blankets around their shoulders and gripping each other's hands for comfort.

A crude pathway led up between some low dunes, illuminated by cold, white moonlight casting curving shadows across it. Hugh walked beside Hanna who'd vacated the bus at the village before his when they'd first arrived. How long ago? Hugh's brain, clouded by a fog of drugs was unable to work it out and although it seemed a long time, he found he was remembering life at home with more clarity than ever. Hanna stumbled. He placed a hand under her elbow as they continued up, rounding a bend so that the bus was lost from view. Ahmed stepped slowly at the head of the column, pausing to wait every now and then in order for his elderly troop to catch up.

At last he stopped where there was a plateau about the size of the garden at the farm, but without the warm familiarity of the old apple tree; without any vestige of life — plant or otherwise. Dunes surrounded them, austere, organic shapes in the moon's glow. Ahmed motioned them to sit and rest after their climb, though there was nowhere but the dusty, flat rock of the plateau and a number of them experienced difficulty in the action, overcoming it by leaning on the more able-bodied until all were down on the ground in various positions. Hugh dropped his blanket down on to the rocky surface then helped Hanna to sit on it before joining her and pulling her blanket around them both.

Ahmed began to show them the stars, pointing out various constellations and explaining their names, but the discourse was not enough to disguise the sound of the bus engine below them. Hugh pulled Hanna's hand on to his lap as she lifted her head in response to the sound. Their guide was instructing them now. "The sunrise from this vantage point," he enthused, "will be the most beautiful sight you will ever see. This is our gift to you, my friends. Please enjoy it. And don't forget your water and your packets when you need them."

Hugh squeezed his companion's hand and noticing the tears on her face felt his own cheeks to be wet. The most beautiful sight to him would be that of his own family, his beloved daughter and son-in-law, his adored granddaughter and the daughter he'd sought to welcome back, as well as his treasured farmhouse on the hillside where he grew up. No view would ever be as dear to him as his home.

He glanced around at the others. They were all huddled together, finding comfort in each other, silent except for coughs or moans of discomfort. When he looked back, their guide had disappeared, silent and stealthy as a wraith he'd crept away to join the bus.

It was late in the afternoon when PAM informed Laura that Hugh was messaging. She'd stayed up working at the screen, going through some figures on fuel costs. She paged Joshua as a blurry image began to materialise.

"It's not defined." She was frowning as he entered the office. "Look, the image is broken up and his voice is there but I can't understand what he's saying."

Josh peered at the space where Hugh ought to be. His shape was moving, fluctuating but pixelated and although they could hear his voice the sounds were too indistinct to understand. He gesticulated, his eyes wild, arms flaying. He appeared to be shouting, his mouth a silent pump of words.

"It must be the signal." Josh fiddled with the settings, achieving no improvement. Outside the wind maintained its customary whistle, further hampering their efforts to hear Hugh, whose movements indicated agitation, the staccato bursts of sound holding some insistence. After a few minutes his appearance became clearer and they could make out words. The old man — for he did appear much older now — was troubled. That he'd become frail was apparent even in the fragmented and intermittent views they were receiving. They leaned forwards to catch the splinters of image and sound they could perceive.

"…not what you think…"

Josh screwed up his face. "What, Hugh? What's not what we think?"

"…the wars…"

"Wars? Which wars? What do you mean?"

Laura sat bolt upright; the skin of her face ashen as she stared at the fluctuating representation of her father. Was he succumbing to dementia, as her mother Ellen had? He was speaking again. "Contrived…"

"Do you mean the African wars, Hugh? When all the deals were made?"

The image appeared to contort, as if Hugh was summoning every particle of energy he could muster. "In their interests…"

"Dad! What are you saying?" Laura held her hands out to the dancing ghost that was her father's likeness. Joshua placed a hand on her arm.

"I don't know if he can hear us. Maybe the signal is poor both ways. Whose interests, Hugh? Africa's?"

The old man continued. In a moment of clarity, the representation became visible and they could make out the extent of Hugh's frailty in the haggard pallor of his face and the tremor in his fingers. "You must join the activists. Join the Organisation. The only way." His body shook. He was attempting to shout. The image degraded, disappearing for a moment before returning as he was mid-sentence. "They'll take everything!"

"Who'll take everything, Dad?"

"...of value — until it is all gone." There was a sudden burst of clarity and they saw the stark intensity in his rheumy eyes.

"We love you, Dad!" Laura cried. There was a hissing sound of static as the image clouded, lost in a deluge of white bars. Then he was gone.

Laura sat still, hand across her mouth, staring into the space where he had been. When she spoke her voice was cracked, the words halting. "What's happened, Josh? Why can't he hear us?"

He looked at her. "He looked as if he was trying to warn us. He must have discovered something. *'not what it seems'*. Did you hear that? Darling, I don't want to frighten you but I have a bad feeling about this. When was the last time we spoke to him?"

"It was a couple of weeks ago, wasn't it? It's been harder to find the time since Farlow... we've been short-handed, and then Jack came. Josh, do you think Dad is OK? I mean, I know he's old now, but they've been looking after him, haven't they? It's what they're meant to do!"

Joshua was frowning. "One thing, we don't know if this broadcast was live, do we? If he couldn't respond to us, converse, it may have been a recording. So, we've no idea when he made this message."

"Can't we find out? It must be annotated with date

and time, surely?"

"PAM, confirm message time and date, please."
There was a pause then PAM's light flashed.

"No data found with the message. Repeat: no data."

Josh tried again. "PAM — replay please." Again,
they waited. After a moment the light flashed.

"Message unobtainable. Please refer to your
computer for more information."

Laura fell on the keyboard, her fingers fumbling in
frantic haste but it was hopeless. The message could not
be called up.

Away in the African desert the sun was flooding the
sky with blood red. Hugh squeezed Hanna's hand. "It's
time," he murmured. "Do you have your packet?" As
she turned her face to his he touched the tears that
streamed down her cheek and knew he was weeping too.
In a simultaneous movement they tipped down the
contents of the phials in their packets, swallowed a few
mouthfuls of water and laid themselves down upon the
flat, hard rock, holding each other as the unforgiving
sun rose in the sky.

Hooper and Uzza

Hooper stood Fulmar offshore. She'd arrived a full twenty-four hours ahead of schedule despite the gusting winds and squalls that buffeted the small craft and was now having some difficulty keeping steady in the conditions. At hourly intervals she went up on deck to scan the crumbling remains of the old port and the refinery for glimpses of her charge but as the light faded, she gave in and retired below to practise some more on her writing.

She was as yet undecided on the other woman's proposition. For most of her adult years she'd opted for what she considered an easy life; for freedom and solitude and to be as much her own boss as was possible nowadays. To commit to joining this organisation was to ruffle the calm surface of her existence. She'd be, to an extent, taking 'orders'. And yet she felt an obligation to the planet and to herself; a compulsion to contribute in some way, anything to hinder the way the earth was sleepwalking its way to destruction. During the last two weeks she'd spent most of her spare time researching and reading and had been shocked at some of the facts she'd discovered, like how much of the earth's surface had been forest and how much had been ice. Still more shocking was the acreage of inhabitable land that had been rendered useless by poison, drought or flood. Man had become the architect of his own demise and seemed unable, now, to undo the damage.

The gales kept up throughout the night and she made regular trips up on to the deck to check the masts, ensure everything was battened down tight. At first light she made her first foray to look for Uzza, using the ancient field glasses to scan back and forth along the old quay. Clinging on to Fulmar's rail with one hand she thought she could make out movement on the rickety platform. Several figures, insect-like, walking or stationary were there. But would Uzza be one of them? It was impossible to tell from this distance. She descended through the companionway, donned her bio-suit and made preparations to bring Fulmar in to the quayside, although as yet she'd no idea whether any of the figures were Uzza and despite having brought supplies for the inhabitants of the Wastelands there was no way to ascertain what kind of welcome there would be.

She gunned the engine and made a slow approach, wary that at any time she would need to manoeuvre the boat around and get away fast. As she drew nearer, she could see that there three or four standing people and a couple seated, plus one that was lying horizontal upon an area of the decking that had not collapsed. The prone body, dressed in a white suit was Uzza. Was she sleeping? Dead? Hooper swallowed and narrowed her eyes, gripping Fulmar's wheel hard as she pressed her on towards the appointed rendezvous.

At last she was alongside, bobbing in the choppy

waves that lapped against the disintegrating framework of the jetty. As she lowered the engine's throb to idling there was an abrupt jerk as a hook caught the craft's rail and pulled her in. Glancing out she caught a glimpse of legs clad in ragged trousers. There would be no withdrawal now, she thought and taking a deep breath she ascended the ladder to the deck. The four standing people stepped forwards. Uzza — for it was her — was lying on her back a few metres away between two others, seated. There was little to indicate whether the people were men or women except that some had straggly beards. Hooper, deciding to take the initiative indicated the boxes she'd placed beside her on the deck, hoping this would lead to some spirit of cooperation and the nearest Wastelander nodded, beckoning her. She lifted a box and lobbed it over, stumbling a little as the waves bounced Fulmar against the jetty then reached for another. The boxes were righted and stacked by one of the others. She opened her arms to show there were no more and was beckoned once more to suggest that she herself must now disembark. With misgivings and a thumping chest she stepped up off Fulmar, which by now had been secured to the rickety landing stage and lunged for the nearest bit of decking, where her arm was caught and she was hauled up by the leading Wastelander on to the platform where she stood facing him and was able to scrutinise at close hand for the first time.

Though he was thin and unkempt he appeared to be

defect-free, although several of the others had obvious physical abnormalities such as cloudy eyes and mal-formed features. How old was he, she wondered? His gaze was unwavering as he stood whipped by the wind and lashed by the squall, rain wet on the leathery skin of his cheeks and they stood for several moments like this until Hooper broke the spell, motioning in the direction of the prone woman, who she now realised was under some kind of guard where she lay inert, battered by the wind and rain. She could not tell if the woman was alive, but there didn't appear to be an obvious injury and her suit and breathing apparatus were intact. Hooper shifted on her feet, looking in Uzza's direction. The two guards, women perhaps as they had no facial hair, stood and shuffled to pick her up, showing, Hooper noted, a degree of tenderness in the careful way they held her; one cradling her head as it lolled on to her chest, the other holding fast under her lower legs. They shuffled towards Fulmar and the skipper returned to the deck in order to bring Uzza on board. The Wastelander holding the boat hook held fast as they manoeuvred round and edged the woman's body on to the bobbing deck, where Hooper pulled her around to fit into the space. The Wastelander women withdrew back on to the jetty, stepping back to join their companions as the hook was withdrawn and Fulmar released, rocking from side to side. Hooper left Uzza on deck and wasted no time in starting the engine as two Wastelanders knelt to propel the boat away from the side then she drew away leaving

203

them standing watching, motionless and silent as the ghost of the refinery in the background behind them.

Once she was away from shore, she risked a look at her passenger who had not stirred or opened her eyes but was breathing. She manhandled her with as much care as the space would allow until she was below and began to remove the suit, stowing it quickly into a bag before removing her own then sealing the bag for fumigation later. She lifted Uzza on to the small seat inside the cabin, opened the medicine kit and set up a fluid line before making the basic checks. Having found no injury or sickness, Hooper could only assume that Uzza had either ingested a poisonous substance or that drugs had been administered to her. In either case there was no more that could be done until they reached medical facilities.

Hooper placed a heat-retaining cover over the woman and turned her attention to navigating Fulmar towards European waters.

Later in the afternoon, when she came to check on Uzza her eyes were open, although she hadn't moved. She sat opposite her.

"Uzza." The woman's eyes rested on her. "Can you hear me?" She blinked and gave a barely perceptible nod. "Are you feeling sick?" Her lips moved but no sound emitted and she struggled as if to sit up. Hooper lifted a hand. "Don't try to move. I've set up some fluids for now. When we reach mainland, we'll get you to a health centre."

Uzza's eyes widened and she opened her lips to attempt a protest, prompting the captain to relent. "OK — we'll see how it goes. If you get your strength back in a few hours we may not need to, although it would be a good idea to get you looked over since you've been in the deadliest part of the planet for the last two weeks."

By that evening, as they continued their choppy voyage towards Berlin, Uzza had recovered enough to sit up, have her fluid line removed and tell Hooper a little about her experiences in the Wasteland. She was quick to say that the people she'd encountered had been as agreeable and cooperative as their circumstances allowed.

"At first there was a degree of suspicion," she began, "but I showed them the water purification system and gave them some medication from my pack and they seemed to respond with friendship. They have very little. Their shelters are rudimentary and fashioned from the ruins of ancient structures but a place was offered to me for sleeping. They try to grow food but the results are pitiful in the poisonous soil and I suppose anything they've grown is contaminated with poison like everything else." Hooper nodded.

"I saw a handful of children and babies, most with stunted limbs, facial deformities or blindness. The people are able to communicate by unsophisticated speech but I get the feeling that spoken language is dying and they rely more on gesture. I did manage to capture some of their behaviour and society on screen."

Hooper interrupted. "We can look later. You should save your strength for recovery."

"I also took many samples of soil and plants. Some of the plant samples are very disturbing." She reached for her pack, opened it and withdrew a small sample bag containing phials, one of which she held up with tweezers for Hooper's inspection.

"We should be cautious!" her companion told her. "Don't forget that everything you bring out is contaminated!"

Uzza nodded. "I will place the bag into the fumigation chamber in a moment. Do you see this?" She held the small phial up towards the light. It contained a piece of foliage.

"These are leaves taken from a tree which I established to be a juniper, a coniferous shrub very common in this area of Wasteland, which was formerly known as Russia. The Wastelanders use the berries and leaves from this shrub to make infusions, which they believe to have medicinal properties and it may have had healing properties in ancient times. Whether this can be true once the plant is contaminated is debatable. Each leaf should be a glossy green with a narrow grey stripe along the centre." She set her face in a grimace.

Hooper peered at the withered leaves inside the phial. They were the colour of ashes, dusty with a silvery patina, small and shrivelled, unrecognisable as juniper leaves. "What is it, do you think? What is the disease?"

"It is a blight of some kind. I cannot be specific until I have access to a laboratory but I will know more when I have analysed the sample. But it is very worrying."

"Do you have access to a laboratory? How will you do it?"

The woman nodded, smiling. "I am blessed. I have had the good fortune to find a position in a company with very substantial laboratory facilities."

"Where is that, if I may ask?"

"I have been appointed as director of a Greenergy farm and processing works in the UK. The departing CEO is being promoted into government. It is just the opportunity I was waiting for." She sat back, smiling.

"Isn't that dangerous? What if the company finds out you are working for this, 'organisation'?"

Uzza smiled again and nodded, then yawned. "I expect it is. But I am not planning for anyone to find out. And you are not going to tell anyone, are you, Hooper?"

The skipper shook her head. "That is what I thought. You see I am a good judge of character." And with that she lay down on the bench and closed her eyes.

Earthsend

Holly ran in through the kitchen without shedding her Parka or boots, calling. "Mum? Where are you?" And, receiving no reply, she moved on through to the small office where her mother was often ensconced at this time of day. Jack trailed behind her, uncertain now that it had been wise to impart his revelatory information. At the time it had felt good to know things and be proved right but the sharing of secrets had provoked an ominous panic in Holly and now it felt like he'd opened a sluice gate and an overflow was about to begin.

She'd stopped in the office doorway. Looking past her into the tiny room he could see Laura, seated at the desk, her head covered by her hands and Joshua standing with his arms around her. Holly appeared to be paralysed by the scene. He tugged at the back of her coat. "Maybe now is not the best time," he mumbled, but she ignored him.

"Mum!"

Her father looked round, tears welling. "Shh! Holly, your Mum's had a shock." Holly moved towards them.

"What's happened? Is Mum sick?"

Josh indicated the remaining chair, just inside the

door. "Sit down, Holly. We have bad news about your granddad. We think he may have been taken to rest without our knowledge."

Holly's face turned ashen. "Dad! What do you mean?"

Her father turned from Laura and squatted down in front of his daughter, catching her hands in his. "PAM sent a message through from him, but it wasn't live. It had been recorded weeks ago. We don't know how it got sent. We think he was trying to tell us, although the transmission was faulty and difficult to understand."

She stared at him; eyes wild. "No. You don't know. It must be a mistake. They look after the elders there. He told me himself. They are caring people… religious. They wouldn't hurt him. He was helping them, teaching the children…"

"Holly! Holly, listen. I'll show you something." He left her and went to the console. "PAM, news bulletin from seventeen hundred hours, please."

There was a gathering of people on some steps in front of a building, smiling and posing for the press.

"In an historic, unprecedented move, agreement has been reached between energy giants Greenergy and SOL for a merger. Talks have been underway since Senate gave the go-ahead last June when Greenergy made a bid to acquire SOL and all its assets, including water pipelines and solar power transfers. Under new conditions, several arrangements that were made under the treaty of 2175 will no longer be valid, including the

transfer and care of elders to the solar fields and the reciprocal voluntary work that has been carried out. SOL spokesman, Rashid Affur, confirmed that an agreement to care for elders currently residing in the Margins of solar fields would be honoured but that no more elderly citizens would be transported to their villages.

Greenergy's European representative to Senate, Axel Berenson, revealed that plans to bring wind power under the umbrella, Zephyr, were underway and talks were due to begin next January. The new global company is to be called Element. Newly appointed Element PR head, Marcia Stein, outlined plans for the company to expand into food production."

As the European Parliament correspondent moved in on Marcia for an interview, Joshua made an abrupt move and switched the bulletin off. There was silence in the crowded office. Jack shuffled his feet as he leaned in the doorway.

"They're not religious. There's no religion, not really. It was only ever about control, that's what my Dad says, anyway."

Josh and Holly gazed at him. Both looked bewildered. Laura had not lifted her head from her hands. Her husband stood and placed an arm around her shoulders. "We'll find out what's happened to Hugh. There must be a way to get to the truth. They made this deal at the end of the African Wars as part of the contract for housing SOL. They agreed to look after the elders so that's what they must do! I said I'd never speak to Berenson again but I'll need to grit my teeth and go over there…"

"He's not there." There was nothing triumphant in Jack's impassive tone.

"It's true, Dad! We went over there. It was what we came in to tell you. And you've seen for yourself on the bulletin now, anyway. He's left to become a government representative or something. There's someone else there — a woman. And we found something else out…" Holly's flushed face turned towards Jack, who was unable to meet her look. He folded his arms.

"Well, I didn't want to bother you with it, but I knew ages ago that dog handler guy was working at Berenson's farm."

Laura raised her head, her face puffy and wet. "I don't understand," she whispered.

"Mum, Jack told me the dog guy could have stopped the dogs from attacking if he'd wanted to. He has some kind of gadget that shocks them. So why didn't he stop them killing Farlow?"

"Josh," Laura pleaded. "What are we going to do? None of us is safe here any more." He closed his arms more tightly around her.

"I assumed the handler had run for it to avoid prosecution for neglect. I had no idea he was there, next door, free as a bird!"

Laura shrugged him off and swivelled towards the

console. "I'll get on to the police right away," she blurted but her husband held her hands in his.

"Laura, don't you see? This man, this perpetrator of murder, is being sheltered on a farm which, until recently at least, has been run by someone who's been promoted into Parliament. Parliament runs the police force. What do you think the Police will do? My guess is nothing at all." He turned back. "Jack…" he began, but the boy had gone.

"Dad, we'll have to tell Ethan." Joshua nodded at his daughter. "Shall I message him?"

He shook his head. "No, only to ask him to come over. They should all come, if they can. We must tell them together, here."

There had been a quiet acknowledgement that Ethan, Ewa and Kav were now a unit and they had all made an unremarked move into Ewa's little cottage. Hoping not to alarm Ethan, Joshua tried to keep his voice even and calm as he messaged his adopted son and asked him to bring Ewa and Kav over to the farmhouse as there was something they should know. Ethan was curious but agreed they would come as soon as he'd completed spraying in tunnel thirty-four, been home, changed and made sure Kav wasn't napping. Josh left Laura and Holly and went to make tea for them all, hoping a hot, sweet drink might help them overcome the shock they were experiencing.

Hugh's comfortable living room with its squashy sofas and walls lined with old books was where the subdued family assembled. Ewa handed Kav to Holly as she took Laura in her arms. The baby squealed with pleasure and made grabs for the red strands of hair that framed the girl's face and she buried her nose in his tiny neck to inhale the soothing, innocent essence of him.

Ethan had, at first, been speechless at the news of his grandfather and of the revelation that Farlow's death had been murder but now he was angry. "We can't sit back and let these companies manipulate our lives! They can't be allowed to get away with anything they like! That's two murders they are responsible for. Those were people we loved, people who were part of our lives. We have to do something. We won't be the only ones to have been treated this way. We have to fight them — fight the company. Futura is moored down there in the harbour, just waiting for me. I've been here too long anyway. I'll take the fight to them, in Basel. I'll go tomorrow morning at first light."

Ewa spoke to him, her voice soft. "Ethan, I don't know what you think can be done, but Kav has lost one father and I have lost one husband. I don't think our hearts can take any more breaking. We all need you to be here. Kav and I need you and Laura, Josh and Holly need you, too."

Joshua stood at the window, staring as clouds of drizzle blew across the garden, almost obliterating the apple tree. Hugh's neglected vegetable beds displayed little evidence of the tender care they had received under his dogged devotion. Undeterred by lashing rain and buffeting winds he'd be out there pulling out unwanted rape plants, administering fertiliser, staking and tying whatever the conditions.

"We could start by trying this woman who has taken over from Berenson, whoever she is. She may have a better idea about what's happened. We need to meet her anyway, although my feeling is, we can't trust anyone employed by an energy company. What *would* be useful though, Ethan, is if you come with me to see her. I'd ask you, Laura, but for now I think it's best if you stay here and get some rest. Ewa, there is some sedative in Hugh's bathroom cabinet. Can I ask you to take care of her for me?"

The young woman nodded, looked back at Laura and pushed a strand of wet hair away from her cheek. "We'll stay around for now," she murmured. On her other side, Holly rocked to and fro with Kav in her arms, humming to him and gazing into his rapt face.

Joshua strode back through to the office. "PAM, get me Greenergy Longhope please." He waited for a moment.

"Sorry, Joshua. Greenergy is no longer a valid contact. Please advise action."

Ethan had followed him into the office. "Already?" he asked. "They haven't wasted much time, have they? You'll have to ask for 'Element', Josh. That's what they're calling themselves now, isn't it?"

"PAM, get me Element Longhope, please." There was a click before the automated message told him he was through to reception and invited him to select from the options. He screwed up his face. "We never had all this before when Berenson was there!" Ethan shrugged.

"I'll hold," Josh told the virtual messenger. In the meantime, they were treated to a loop of film showing them the wonders of the bio-fuel plant, voiced over with a smooth commentary extolling the achievements of the firm and how much more could be achieved now that it had become associated with the success story that was SOL. They watched with growing disgust.

"Fuck this!" shouted Josh and killed the screen to begin again. This time he opted for 'customer', waited again and after several minutes was talking to customer service operator, Carl, seated in a booth. "I want to speak to the boss."

"May I take your name, please?"

"I am Joshua Conway. My wife and I own the food production company next door."

"And what did you want to order?"

"I don't want to order anything, I…"

"I'm sorry. I'm afraid you are through to orders. Which department did you want?"

"I want to speak to the head of operations there! She's a new woman, taken over from Berenson."

Carl's bland features displayed no emotion. "May I ask what this is about?"

Josh drew as close as he could to the man's image before barking. "No! You may not ask!"

There was a pause; the service operator remained

impassive as he replied. "I can put you through to the CEO's admin department. You may be able to make an appointment to speak to someone from there."

Joshua moved to switch him off but Ethan pressed a hand to his arm, saying "OK, we'd like to make an appointment. Please put us through."

They waited. "Can you tell us the name of the new CEO?" Ethan asked the admin officer, a sallow, gaunt woman, hair scraped away into a tight ponytail. Joshua stared. He recognised none of these people, and yet he'd been a frequent visitor to Greenergy Longhope until a few weeks ago, on nodding terms with many of the workers there. Were they still employed there? The woman was looking at her screen as she spoke. So far, she'd not as much as glanced in their direction.

"Element Longhope is run by Uzza Farzul." She continued to consult the screen. "Her diary for the coming week is full, but she may be able to offer you an appointment during the following week. That would be the week beginning on the twenty-first."

Joshua moved quickly and switched the messenger off. "Let's go!" he said.

"Josh, is that wise? They may just put security on to us."

"I don't care. I'm going over there. I'd like you to come, Ethan, but I'll understand if you don't."

"No, you can't go alone. I'll come." The young man went back to the women. "We're going over now," he told them.

"She said she'll see you?" Ewa's eyes were wide.

"Yes, she'll see us tonight. We're going now." And he hurried to catch up with Joshua, who was already out of the house.

Element Longhope

They took the farm truck, Joshua driving. Visibility was poor as billowing mizzle obliterated the rocky track. In places deep ruts made negotiating the path tricky. Joshua cursed as the wheels snagged and spun in yet another hole. "This road's got a lot worse. I haven't been up here by truck for a while."

"You've had other stuff to deal with. I can take a look at it tomorrow if you want."

"Don't worry, Ethan. It isn't a priority. Let's get all this mess sorted out first."

Expecting to be stopped by security, Joshua made a slow approach to the entrance gates, over which surveillance drones patrolled in a continuous loop, day and night. They would know by now that he and Ethan were on their way. While giant floodlights illuminated the gateway and the drones continued to appear and disappear overhead, the enormous, reinforced metal rectangles were wide open. Josh halted the truck outside.

"Why are the gates open, do you think? Is it a trap?"

Ethan touched his shoulder. "They'll have known we were coming, that's all. You're bound to feel suspicious but let's go and find out what this Uzza woman has to say. I bet she's expecting us. That's why the gates are open."

As the truck rolled through the gap into the courtyard the huge gates swung shut behind them in a silent sweep. Rain was cascading across the neat, paved quadrangle and running from the downpipes into efficient channels that carried it out of harm's way. There was no one about, although eyes on stalks followed the two men as they got out of the vehicle and walked towards the main door of a lit building. The door opened as they approached and a courteous, disembodied voice welcomed them to 'Element', inviting them to please wait and someone would attend to them. The two glanced at each other as they stood in the hallway. Ethan felt that the voice had a curious, transatlantic intonation as though a hybrid.

At last they heard footsteps, light and swift, approaching from a corridor to the right of the stairs and a slim woman appeared wearing a dark tunic, and trousers, her hair covered with an elegant black scarf. She faced them, a faint smile on her lips and affected a slight bow of greeting.

"Good evening. Allow me to introduce myself. I am Uzza Farzul and I have been appointed head of this facility. And you are our neighbours, Dr Joshua Conway and Mr Ethan Conway. Is that correct? I have heard about you," she regarded Ethan, "from our mutual friend, Captain Hooper." She held out a slender, brown hand, the fingers narrow and delicate. Joshua blinked at the use of his title, gained from university study, and was conscious of his own, large, calloused hand as he took hers. Her skin was warm and smooth. She greeted Ethan in the same way and asked them to follow her back along the corridor the way she had come.

She led them into a comfortable living room, furnished with a couple of modern sofas, a colourful rug, a coffee table and a wall console. On another wall behind them there was a large painting depicting a landscape of forests and mountains. Joshua glanced around. He had never been into this part of the complex, having always met Berenson in an upstairs office. This must be the woman's living quarters. Uzza motioned them to sit, then sat herself opposite them, upright and neat, hands in her lap.

"May I offer you some refreshment?" she asked. "Some tea or a beer?"

Joshua shook his head and leaned forwards, hands on his knees. "We've come for some answers, Ms Farzul…"

"Please, it's Uzza. We are neighbours after all. And I will call you Joshua, if I may?"

"My father-in-law, Hugh Conway, travelled to the SOL fields three months ago under the agreement that was made in the African Pact. My son here, Ethan, transported him himself. He was happy and optimistic, looking forward to his retirement and the task he was to do, teaching horticulture skills to their children. Up until a month ago we received regular v-messages from him showing us his life there in the Margins, his home, his garden and the children he instructed. Then the messages became less frequent. Now we've had a disturbing message that seems to be recorded. He is upset. He tries to tell us something is very wrong. We've no idea where he is and we think that SOL may have terminated him. Your company is involved with SOL. We don't know who else can help us." He sat back, staring at the woman opposite him.

Her level gaze met his for a moment then she dropped her head a little in a small nod. "This is very distressing, a terrible thing for you and your family, Joshua. I know the company has promised to honour its commitments to the elders in this respect. As you know I've only recently arrived here since the merger of Greenergy and SOL so these first few weeks is concerned with fact finding and settling in. At the moment all I can do is promise to find out what I can. If what you say is true and SOL has reneged on its agreement to care for our older folk, it will have been a very serious breach of the treaty indeed, a scandal."

Ethan glanced at his father then spoke. "There is another issue. You have a man working here who is responsible for the murder of our farm co-worker, Farlow James."

Uzza's eyes widened. "There is a murderer residing here, at this facility?"

Ethan studied her. The disclosure had shaken her. She rose and went to an ornate, rosewood desk in a corner of the room. Pulling out a drawer she withdrew a small paper book and from the top she took a real pen before returning to sit as before. She opened the book to a page where there was no writing and wrote by hand on the clean, white rectangle.

"Please," she said. "Tell me what you know."

Ethan related the events of the night of the attack and of what Jack and Holly had seen. She wrote in quick strokes without interrupting him or dismissing the facts because they were witnessed by young children. When he'd finished, she looked up. "Hooper was very complimentary about you, Ethan. She told me you were sincere, reliable and a hard worker. She was reluctant to take you on at first but she could not have found a better seaman or a braver one. She would rather sail alone than work with anyone else. I've spent some time with her and I know I can rely on her judgement.

"All I can say tonight, gentlemen, is that I will be making these issues a priority. First thing tomorrow I shall find out if this man..." she consulted her notes, "Porc, is residing here at the plant. Then I will contact my Element colleagues in the solar fields and make enquiries about your father-in-law, Hugh. You did the right thing coming here and bringing the issues to my attention." She sighed. "In confidence, I do have concerns regarding the company and there are issues I will not be able to fix. I will need to discuss these with you at a later date, but I suggest tonight is not the appropriate time."

She walked them back to the entrance, pausing to shake their hands once more. "May I message you in the next few days, Joshua, to arrange another meeting? I know you and your family will need time to adjust to the situation you are in."

He nodded. "Thank you for seeing us. I'm sorry we…"

She held up a hand. "You have no need to apologise. It is I — we who should feel shame, we the company."

As they pulled out of the yard the giant gate swung closed behind them. The rain had ceased but a fierce wind pummelled the farm truck as they drove back along the hillside track. Falling debris from above meant slow progress. Ethan grimaced as the wheels snagged on boulders brought down in the latest drop. "You wouldn't think there would be anything left to come down, would you? There's no soil remaining up here, only bare rock. Where does it all come from?"

"It's getting worse, Ethan. Haven't you noticed? The rainfall is heavier and the gales are fiercer than ever. Now there's no soil left up here, nothing to bind the rock, nothing for plants to hang on to, nothing to stop it all breaking off and tumbling down. We are spending more of our time on repairs and protection and less on growing food. I don't know what we can do. We're running around like sprayed aphids and maybe we are as doomed as they are."

Ethan noted the despair in Joshua's voice and felt

vulnerable and exposed. He'd never heard his adopted father speak like this. As he was growing up, Josh had been a strong, kind, stable parent, the man he'd idolised, the man who had allowed him to grow and follow his passion for the sea. Now he seemed defeated, his devotion to his chosen profession shaken. Then there was Laura, broken by this news of Hugh issuing on top of the heartache of losing Farlow. He swallowed, feeling the weight of responsibility settling down upon his shoulders, wanting more than ever to escape, to return to the one place where he felt in control and yet knowing he could not — would not — abandon his family at this time.

"At least this woman, Uzza, seems to want to help us. Perhaps the new company will be able to assist the hillside farmers, Josh. We are not the only ones struggling to survive, are we? Food producers do vital work that communities cannot survive without. There must be a way that the energy company can work with us, especially if they are forming part of the European government. They'll have to, otherwise people won't get fed."

Joshua was silent, negotiating the last part of the track that led to their yard. The wind, furious in its assault, hectored them as they strove to open the doors and dash to the shelter of the farm porch.

They shed their coats and walked through to Hugh's living room, where only Ewa and Holly remained, the baby asleep in the girl's arms now as the three sat together on the sofa. Their upturned faces were eager, probing as the men walked in.

"Dad!" Holly closed her eyes for a moment. "We were so worried!"

Joshua sank down on the other side of his daughter, placed his arm around her and planted a kiss on her cheek. He stroked the top of Kav's downy head. "It's OK. We are fine. Where is your mother?"

"I got her to bed. She was exhausted." Ewa looked over the top of Holly at him then stood to put her arms around Ethan, who folded her up in a hug. Outside the gale whistled, threatening the fabric of the old house; ominous grinding and bumping sounds issuing from above.

"What happened, Dad?" Holly's eyes blazed and her cheeks were flushed. He pulled her closer.

"Don't think about it now. Tomorrow we'll gather up and have a family conference. I think we all need to sleep."

"We will all stay here tonight, Joshua. It's best we are together." Ewa looked up at Ethan, who nodded. She took the baby from Holly, who allowed her father to shepherd her towards the stairs. As they ascended, they were aware of a repeated banging somewhere outside the walls. Holly paused on a stair.

"Something's come loose," she said. Joshua nodded.

"We'll look in the morning. Come on — to bed."

225

Uzza

Uzza went to her desk and brought up some files to the screen, flicking through still images then drone surveillance footage. At last she stopped a sequence, running it back a little until she could see the figure, a thick-set, swarthy man with a mane of black hair. He was entering one of the outhouses.

She sat back. The man had not been amongst the assembled employees she'd called together when she arrived, of this she was sure. She checked the personnel files, picture IDs, employment histories and personal details. Nobody resembled this man. He had not only left the establishment but his file had been erased. Where was he now? And where had he come from? Berenson must have hired him but it seemed unlikely that he'd be in his employ now that the previous Greenergy boss had been elevated to government status.

She got out her pen and paper and began a letter.

S

I believe you have previously had dealings with a man known as 'Porc'. I am interested in tracking this man down and need any information you may have on his whereabouts. The matter concerns members of your family.

U

She tucked the note into an envelope before writing 'S' and the number '2' on to the front. She turned the envelope over, withdrew a small red block from her drawer and heated it with a bio-fuel flame until it melted, dropping a tiny, glistening blob on to the v-shaped join at the back. This action gave her a curious satisfaction as she watched the wet blob drying to a hard seal. Sometimes there could be no substitute for the ancient ways.

She took a few minutes to erase her search history before shutting down the screen and switching everything off, taking the envelope and tucking it into a fold of her headscarf. She left the office and padded barefoot along the corridors of the cavernous Element building, taking a lift to the staff quarters — small but comfortable self-contained units overlooking the rape fields. She knocked softly on a door. A young, blond man opened it a slit then seeing her, let her in.

"Ralph, I need you to get this note to this recipient as quickly as possible." She withdrew the envelope to show him where S2 was clearly written. Ralph smiled.

"Shouldn't be a problem. Any ideas where S2 could be?"

"Last we knew he was based in Longhope, but he left as the virus was taking hold. He'd been living with a partner; Cath Regis is her name. She got sick and went to quarantine. We think he's gone north but we've heard nothing from him for a while. He'd been getting to know the agitators to try and find out who were company moles. I think this Porc character was employed by Berenson and his protestor persona was a front. Basically, he is a thug, a henchman hired to undermine small enterprises such as the Conways."

Ralph nodded. "There is a network of cells I can use for enquiries. I'll take a boat at first light."

"You may be able to get Hooper if she's available. You could try messaging her tonight. No need to discuss the reason for travel."

"No. All right, I'll try her." He took the envelope.

"Ralph, stay safe."

His eyebrows rose. She'd never warned him before. He grinned but she frowned back.

"I mean it. We're going to need you more than ever in the next months if what I think is going to happen transpires."

By first light he was down by the quayside, buffeted by gusts as he boarded Fulmar. The compact taxi-boat bucked and rocked in its mooring and Hooper stepped forward to assist him in.

Uzza went to the lab and donned her white suit. She unlocked the combination on the cold store and took out her samples, taking them to the bench and holding them up to the light before turning on the powerful microscope equipment. She placed the phial with the juniper leaf into a glass box, manipulating it remotely to snip a small sample for examination. She soon became absorbed in her investigation. How long? How long would it take the disease to arrive here?

She was under no illusions about Element. If she knew about the blight then so did the company. Berenson had already jumped ship and must have known what was coming. She bit her lip. The yellow expanse of oil seed rape fields, obnoxious as they were to Joshua Conway, may even now be harbouring the first signs of spores. She'd need to get out and make a thorough inspection as soon as possible.

But what would this mean for the Conways's farm? She sighed, resting her chin on her hands. The last months had been hard enough on them as it was. And while the tunnels offered some degree of protection from the spores, it could only be a matter of time before the crops became infected.

She stood and walked to the window to stare at where the sickly early morning light seeped over the colourless expanse of rape, bilious gusts of drizzle peppering the glass. How was anyone going to eat, live or survive?

Berenson

Around the table the mood was sombre. Eleven senators sat, like Berenson, screens at their disposal, although Head of State was bombarding them with images, footage and facts, demanding all of their attention.

The situation, he told them was serious. Around the globe the best scientists were working around the clock to analyse the blight spores but as yet no antidote, no pesticide or anti-fungal substances had been found to have an impact on this most pernicious and deadly infection. And while it appeared to have originated in the Wastelands, the spores had been discovered throughout the Eastern sector; areas such as Turkey, Albania and Greece were all affected.

A sequence of images revealed the range of crops that had been damaged, Mediterranean staples, many of them. These were crops that still grew in the open without the need for tunnels, the areas considered margins, corridors between storm-ravaged Northern Europe and the bleached, blistering deserts of Africa and the East.

"Do we know where the blight originated?" asked the man on Berenson's right, Raj Patel. There was a pause. Head of State dipped his chin and ran a hand through his mop of white hair before looking up around the room and clearing his throat.

"We have no proof as yet, but the most likely suggestion is that it has been born of pollution. Breeds of bacteria appear to have developed that feed on the poison in our atmosphere, in our soils and in our seas. The blight may have evolved from this process."

The members were shocked. Raj persisted. "But for decades we've had strategies in place to mitigate the effects of pollution. We no longer use fossil fuels. We limit travel. We have striven to produce the cleanest, least damaging power sources, we…"

Head of State broke in, holding up a hand. "Yes. Yes. All of this is true. Technology has advanced a long way and all of the innovations and strategy decisions were correct, my friend. But here is the thing. Despite all the recognition, the policy making, the sacrifices, the innovation and agreements of the last hundred years, one immovable, undeniable, grave fact remains. It was all too late. We must, every one of us face this, my friends. The damage that the human race has done to planet earth cannot be reversed."

A woman on Berenson's left, Chimanda, leaned forward, squinting at the picture of shrivelled and blackened olives, their leaves crinkled and blotched.

"Surely," she began, "the crops in these areas can be protected by tunnels such as those used in Northern Europe?"

"Tunnels may delay or limit the extent and spread

of the blight," replied the French delegate, "but as yet there is no means of destroying the spores and it would only be a matter of time before the tunnels were breached. We consider that investment of tunnels to these areas is not cost effective."

There was silence throughout the conference room as the delegates took this in. Berenson glanced around at his colleagues. He'd made his move out of agriculture. That was all that mattered.

Chimanda's eyes, wide and intense, fixed on the delegate opposite her. "How then is food production to continue?"

Around the room Berenson noticed many more stricken expressions. This must be news to them. The Frenchman spread his hands and gave a barely perceptible shrug. "Of course, every laboratory will be working full-tilt to find a solution to the blight problem; but in the mean-time we have to draw on stored harvests from less polluted areas."

Head of State raised a hand. "I must move on, if I may. In the light of the blight's progress towards Northern Europe I propose that we cut Greenergy loose from the Element umbrella. This would seem the most prudent course of action given that the likelihood of the rapeseed oil crop becoming damaged will render it no longer profitable."

Concurrence was clear in the nods and murmuring throughout the room, Berenson nodding along with them and allowing himself an inward smirk, thinking of

Uzza, the woman who'd replaced him at the company in Longhope and who would now be redundant.

Chimanda spoke up again. "What arrangements will be made for the workers in that sector?" The others gazed at the woman. Berenson turned to her.

"The vast majority of the workforce has no contract and can safely be dismissed without the need for compensation. Most are seasonal help and taken on when needed. I would expect most senior management to take a sideways step into Zephyr or SOL, wouldn't you say, Chapman?"

There was a ripple of dissent as several members spoke together in low voices. Next to Berenson, Chimanda raised her voice. "I must protest! The practice of letting people go is not ethical nor is it good for business. We are talking thousands upon thousands of people left with no employment." Hands pressed together and eyes blazing she appealed to Head of State Chapman, as she spoke.

Chapman, standing, hands in pockets nodded gently, a small, patronising smile playing on his lips. "I understand and appreciate your concern, Chimanda, and empathy for our workforce is a worthy and laudable emotion, however, all of us must remember that we are not only in governance but employed in running a business and the duty of a business is principally to turn a profit."

Seeing there were nods and whispers of assent at this, Berenson folded his arms and sat back. "There are always the food producers. They'll be needing seasonal help and *more* of it as time goes on and production becomes more difficult. I suggest we become proactive here and go to press with an initiative to divert them into food farms. That way we come across as a humane and sympathetic employer."

The delegates smiled and a few even applauded. Chapman, beaming, looked delighted. "That is an excellent suggestion, Berenson. We'll get the personnel team onto it right away. Any other business? No? Then I think we're about done for now."

Earthsend

The Conways went back to work. What else was there? Most days consisted of a ceaseless round of repairs, vigilance and maintenance as the elements battered and tore into the infrastructure in a relentless bid to destroy the tunnels and their contents.

Joshua got up each morning before everyone else, walking to the fields, bent over into the biting winds, since few days were calm enough to cycle. The family bikes languished in the outhouse, unused.

Some mornings the tall man would straighten, steady himself and look up to the summit of craggy Gethyn Hill, to where the towering turbines revolved in a dizzying display. How long? He would wonder then. How long until they topple? It was well known that their foundations were crumbling, eroded by torrential rains that caused mudslides and mountain avalanches to pour down into Longhope.

Holly was teaching Jack the basics of fruit and vegetable production. Reluctant at first, he'd begun to show an interest, chiefly in the technology aspects of the outfit, was quick to learn and brimming with questions. "Why does anyone need to operate the machine?" he asked, inspecting the pollinator. "Can't it be altered to seek the flower parts itself?"

Laura worried about the children making the trip to the field unaccompanied in unpredictable conditions, persuading them to wait for her each day so that they could all travel together. This constituted unwarranted motherly intervention and control as far as Holly was concerned but she wasn't given a choice.

They worked with Laura inside the tunnels, aided part-time by Ewa, while Josh and Ethan laboured outside in a dogged pursuit of maintenance, securing the frames, battening down the heavy, polythene casings and repairing damage to water and feed hoses. This was how they were all occupied mid-morning when one of Element's dark green, all-terrain vehicles crawled up to the tunnel field and came to a halt.

Rain was driving in a horizontal sweep across the field, reducing visibility and, combined with the wind, causing polythene sheeting that had escaped its anchor to flap like a panicking bird. Ethan was cursing as it flew from his grip yet again and as he stood up to catch it, he spotted the vehicle away across the hillside. "We have a visitor," he messaged everyone, watching as a hunched figure wrestled the door open and got out, bent to the wind and rain, swathed and hooded in a cape-like garment. The figure slammed the door shut and glanced around, fixing on Ethan, to whom she waved. He watched as she made her unsteady progress towards a tunnel entrance and disappeared into it.

They gathered to meet her, cramming together into

the small office where she occupied one of the three chairs, the other two taken up by Laura and by Ewa, Kav on her lap, fidgeting and pulling at her blond hair.

Uzza was now dressed as everyone else, in a white bio-suit, having ditched the cape at the tunnel entrance. "I must apologise," she began, "for arriving without a message. I hope you will understand it is because I must talk to you off-air, in person. What I have to tell you I say in the strictest confidence. No word of it must get out. Do I have your promise?" She gazed into each face in turn and each nodded. Jack eyed Holly, frowning, perplexed and she responded with the slightest of shrugs.

"First of all," continued Uzza, "I know that you are facing the most extreme challenges here on the farm and that these challenges are getting more difficult by the day." There were murmurings and nods of assent. "But I am here to tell you that a worse challenge is on its way. There is no easy way to say it. A blight is coming."

Laura interjected. "A blight? What exactly does that mean?" She screwed up her face and turned to the screen.

"Please, Laura, no. No screens. Please don't use the computer!"

Laura swung back as if slapped. They were all silent, waiting. Uzza went on. "Before I came to Element, I undertook a voyage to the Wastelands to do some research. I'd heard that a new plant disease was taking hold and needed to know more about it.

Unfortunately, this disease is no longer confined to the less inhabited regions of our planet. It spreads by airborne spores. The spores have begun to take hold in the Mediterranean regions and now they have been seen in Europe."

She paused as she watched them struggling with this new information. Laura chewed her lip and looked at Joshua, where he leant against the desk, arms folded. "What does it do?" she asked Uzza. "What are its effects?"

The woman sighed. "I have some samples back at the Element lab. I took some juniper leaves. You are at liberty to come and view them and to see the results of my investigation so far. But it seems likely that, should it take hold, it is able to destroy any crop, having no discernible predisposition towards one crop or another. It wilts foliage, causes mildew, renders vegetables and fruit inedible and unable to flower and seed."

Josh shifted his position, gesturing with his large hand at the computer screen. "Why don't we know about this already?"

Uzza nodded. "It's a fair question. I can only tell you that Senate is anxious to keep this quiet. If the general population were to know — well who knows what would occur? Think of the protests we already have over food and housing costs."

"We'll be OK, though, won't we? We farm in the tunnels and take strict precautions with our bio-safety!"

Holly, Laura noticed, was looking flushed and

spoke in a high, staccato voice. Uzza smiled at the girl. "Holly, I can say that at this very moment the best, most qualified scientists in the world are working day and night to find an answer, an antidote to the disease. I, myself, am directing all my energy and resources towards addressing the problem. But it is *you*, Holly, and *you*, Jack, who are most likely to find the answers."

Jack looked startled to be addressed, and by a stranger who knew his name.

"I am asking you to be vigilant; to look for signs in the outside vegetation and to record them with care. Can you do this?"

Both children nodded solemnly at her.

Ethan coughed. "How long, Ms Farzul? How long do you expect it will be before our tunnels become infected?"

Laura swallowed, finding her throat constricted. Ethan was voicing all their thoughts. Uzza spread her long, narrow fingers and pursed her lips, not meeting their eyes. "Our aim must be to prevent infection reaching the tunnels." She watched them shift, all needing to speak, to protest and she lifted her hands to prevent questions. "Yes, I realise the difficulty. But there is a further matter I have to inform you of. It concerns the company."

Now she had stillness and focus. "As you know, Greenergy, Zephyr and SOL have been merged into one huge empire, Element, a company which now governs as well as providing power. Element has proposed cutting the Greenergy section free from the company because the blight has already begun to impact on rapeseed oil crops around the world, rendering it unprofitable in time. Of course, anyone is at liberty to purchase it but soon everyone will know that it would be financial suicide to take it on. You will need to convert to turbine power from now on, for everything from maintaining the tunnels to fuelling your vehicle."

Josh looked alarmed. She nodded. "It's a lot to take in. Element knows all this and has indicated they will be stepping in to help with conversion and so on. They will also be providing additional labour from the redundant Greenergy workforce."

"At what cost?" Laura's voice sounded dull and stifled in the crowded space. Uzza stood, wanting to be on a level with them.

"I can't parcel this up in any attractive way," she said. "Element is planning to take over food production. This is considered vital to human survival. Your home is safe, for the time being, as are your jobs and your roles in the business. But everything will be commandeered by the government, Element. Everything will belong to them."

She looked around the circle, at the stricken, silent Conways then hung her head.

Longhope

Longhope was a different place. A ghost town, its population reduced by two-thirds.

The tower blocks were in urgent need of repair, the metal stairways having lost rails and steps, chunks of cement missing from their prefabricated structures and large numbers of windows cracked, broken or missing. Constant buffeting by raging winds and torrential rain further damaged them, reducing them to little more than slum accommodation for those few who'd had the dubious good fortune to survive the disease and return from quarantine.

On the quayside, commerce continued in desultory fashion, in a haphazard way, trading having been tempered according to the whims of the weather. On a calm, still day unloading, loading and embarking would take place in a kind of frenzy before the ensuing cyclone winds called it all to a halt. Then there would be silent inactivity until the next, relative period of calm.

At times the goods market could be stocked almost as full as it used to be with a selection of imported items although most of the time the shelves lay half empty, the chiller cabinets humming and brightly lit, containing a few cartons. Meal preparation was haphazard and would be dictated by what was available.

In the Submariner, Reuben polished glasses and buffed the bar for the meagre handful of regulars and occasional seaperson who still patronised the place. Nowadays he lived down there, sleeping in a small store room off the bar area. He'd returned from quarantine to discover he no longer qualified, as a single person, for the home he'd shared with Maynard, which in any case had been plundered and trashed; his partner's beautiful art and handcrafted artefacts had disappeared or been trampled or burnt.

Reuben's handsome, toned body had grown a little flabby now that he no longer spent his spare time lifting weights in the gym. His heart was not in it, nor was the gym itself usable, the machines and equipment long since pilfered or fallen into disrepair.

Josh and Ethan had an hour to spare now that they had stowed their produce into the secure quay warehouse prior to loading and had delivered the local batch into Longhope goods market, so they made their way up a rusting gangway staircase and into the dank, wet corridors of the block that housed the Submariner. Both were sombre as they walked the landings past chipped, peeling doors, remembering the last time they had been there, the gruesome sights, the fetid stench, the animal howling and the heavy pall of despair that had pervaded the place.

They descended the narrow, dark steps to the bar. Inside it was quiet, three mariners at a table nursing pint glasses, murmuring together, and one morose looking elderly man perched on a stool, elbows on the bar counter, clenching his glass. Reuben had his back to them as he cleaned and polished the coffee machine, unaware that they'd entered. Josh coughed.

"Reuben?"

He turned around and froze, cloth in hand, brown eyes wide in his fleshy face. "What? Oh my God, man! Joshua — Jeez — it's good to see you! And Ethan! How's the arm? Did they fix it?" He flapped up a piece of the bar and came through to catch Josh in a tight hug, then Ethan.

"What'll you have? It's on me!"

They opted for beers and perched on stools to sip the watery, metallic tasting concoction that passed for ale.

"So," Joshua put his glass down, "how's business?"

Reuben leaned on the bar, rubbing at an imaginary smear on the glossy surface. Still beautiful, his boyish face was etched now with tiny lines, his eyes haunted and touches of grey dotted his black curls.

"Business is slow, like it is for everyone."

They nodded. "There aren't many left and those that are, well they're all adults and most, like Fitz here," he nodded towards the elderly man as though he couldn't hear, "are getting on a bit."

Joshua placed a hand on his shoulder. "I'm sorry Maynard didn't make it, Reub. He saved Jack's life and none of us will forget it." The barman's eyes glistened

243

and he turned away, back to the coffee machine. Josh glanced at Ethan before speaking again. "Reuben, do you know what happened to Spider and Cath? They were regulars in here, weren't they? And we know Cath was friendly with Maynard. They seemed close, what with Jack spending so much time at your place."

Reub left the machine, came around and pulled a stool up beside the pair. "Spider, he wasn't around when the disease hit. You know, he'd come and go a lot; wheeler and dealer, that's what he is." They nodded. "In our block we seemed to be doing ok. Hardly anyone got sick for the first few days but then, one evening, Cath messaged us saying she felt unwell. She had a high temperature and a headache, couldn't keep nothing down. She asked us to take Jack. We fetched him into ours and he was happy enough. He and May — they loved each other, you know? Not in any improper way, you understand?" Josh nodded. "May was good to Jack. He always wanted kids of his own. We talked about it. But I never wanted to bring a child into a place like this. Once we lost the restaurant, we had nothing to offer a kid, that's what I thought anyway."

Josh put a hand on his arm. "Go on."

"Yes. Well Cath had to stay put and she got sicker. We asked her, where Spider was and she said she didn't know. When we saw she was too weak and sick to get up out of bed May decided he was going in to help her. I begged him not to go but he couldn't sit there and watch her getting worse so he went in, got her cleaned up and into bed, gave her some water. That's when he…"

"He caught it from her," Josh finished. Reuben nodded, swallowing. Ethan was silent, watching, hungry for the story to continue.

"I never saw her in quarantine. We were like, in these little cubicles like cells — not allowed out of them. I never saw anyone for a couple of weeks except a mask at the little window in the door shoving water through a gap and later, when I felt better, something to eat. I recovered and came back to find the apartment had been looted. The Submariner was in a bad state, dirty and trashed but I could save it. Even the stock was still here, locked up, so I moved back in. Couldn't see what else to do. Folks began to come back out of quarantine. I looked for anyone I knew, Cath included, but nobody seemed to know what happened to her. I guess without Jack and Spider she'd have lost her apartment, too."

Ethan was frowning. This was leading nowhere. "Reuben, where do you *think* she has gone?" Reuben looked at the young man whose eyes and mouth were so like Cath's. He shrugged.

"If you want my opinion, I think she'll be wherever *he* is. She'll be with Spider. Always will be."

"And where do you think he is?" Ethan's voice was breathless, whispering.

"I heard he might have struck north. There was talk of them setting up communes up there, free of government control, no rules and stuff."

Ethan's shoulders sagged.

Joshua took another sip of beer. "Did you ever meet a guy called Porc? He's a big, chunky guy with rough skin and a lot of black hair. He'd have hung around with Spider — part of his crowd."

Reuben nodded, "Yeah, I've seen him about. He's still here in Longhope."

"What, you've seen him lately?"

"Yeah. Hey Fitz!" He addressed the old man at the end of the bar. "You know that Porc guy, don't you?"

There was a long moment while they waited, the man seeming not to have heard. Then he coughed, continuing to stare into his glass. When he spoke his voice croaked, as if he was unused to conversation.

"I've seen him down at the warehouses sometimes. He was a dog handler or something for a while, up at the plant, the farm place, or so I heard. There was that accident with the dogs then he gave it up. Nowadays I think he works in the loading bays, odd jobs and such — maybe sleeps down there, too."

Reuben interrupted. "Fitz still does a bit of loading when the weather permits, don't you, mate?"

Josh stared at the old man. "The farm, the one where the accident happened? That's our farm. The guy who was killed? He was like family."

Fitz glared into his glass, frowning. "Seems everyone's lost someone, don't it? And some's lost everyone."

Berenson

In his Basel apartment, looking out of the glass wall that faced the Senate buildings, Berenson cradled a tumbler of whisky, feeling unsettled. He'd had a private v-meet with the boss earlier, a congratulatory conversation in which Chapman hinted at further promotion. This could only mean one thing: vice president of Europe! He sipped the expensive, amber liquid, feeling the burn in his throat and smiled into the window at his reflection. He was still an attractive man, still a catch, a player.

And yet he felt dissatisfied. His on-off affair with Aceline had continued but lately he'd begun to tire of their intermittent couplings that consisted only of sex. Aceline was a beautiful, intelligent, vivacious woman; the only woman he'd got to know who could be his equal in company. She had a great sense of humour, her lacklustre marriage often the subject of deprecating jokes.

He felt no sense of loss for not having had children but he'd begun to wonder if the unsettled feeling meant he needed something — someone — in his personal life. He wasn't getting any younger. Vice presidency, a more public role, would be enhanced were he to appear in images with a glamorous wife on his arm. And marriage need not curtail sexual activity with younger partners provided discretion were employed. There would always be conference jollies and a plentiful supply of beautiful young bodies. Could Aceline be persuaded away from her stultified marriage to boring Victor? The promise of the vice presidency might be a persuading factor. He breathed in and placed his glass of whisky on the coffee table.

"Aceline Millefort," he said into his wrist console, then paused. "No, cancel that."

Aceline was beautiful, yes, and intelligent. She understood the machinations of politics and would be complicit in the methods he would need to undertake to get to the top. But was it prudent to take a wife who knew so much? She'd already cheated on her husband, Victor, and might do the same to him, causing a catastrophic fall in favour. And while beautiful, she could no longer be considered to be in the bloom of youth. Berenson frowned into his whisky and took another sip. It would not be difficult to find a gorgeous young woman who'd be prepared to sell herself into his privileged lifestyle of unlimited travel, wealth, perks and power; a young woman who could be taught the protocols, to keep her mouth shut and her body open.

He grinned. It would be a new project. He'd work on it tomorrow. But these thoughts had aroused him to a point where he'd need some company tonight.

"PAM, escort service."

"What would you like?"

He licked his lips. "A pair, I think. One blond, one brunette. Usual shape."

"They'll be with you in ten minutes."

He went into his dressing room and pulled a robe from the closet before shedding his clothes, then took his whisky into the bedroom, pleased he'd had the foresight to acquire an emperor-sized bed as he manoeuvred himself into its centre.

Earthsend

Laura traipsed along the tunnel to the office, where she flopped into her chair and closed her eyes. It must be time to call it a day. She'd get everyone home then call Josh to find out when he and Ethan would be back before she began the evening meal. She was shutting the screen on her desk down when her wrist console vibrated.

"Laura, Cath for you." Laura froze. Cath!

"Thanks, PAM. Put her on."

Her sister appeared, sitting at some kind of screen; the kind that was used a couple of generations ago for communicating. Cath's face loomed, distorted, a face gaunt and pale.

"Laura?"

"Cath! You're safe! Where are you? Are you well?"

"I'm better. I'm OK."

Cath's voice faded in and out, became indistinct, then boomed, then became faint again.

"So, you're out of quarantine but where are you now? We've been worried sick. Josh and Ethan went to Longhope with the produce and they were going to try and find you."

Cath's eyebrows lifted as she gave her sister a wan smile. "I haven't gone back to Longhope. Why would I? I have nothing there; no job, no partner, no stepson, no apartment and no friends. I've lost the lot, Laura."

Tears sprang to Laura's eyes, hearing the familiar guilt-inducing tone. "Come to us! Jack's here now, and Ethan! There's more than enough work here, Cath! Please, come and live with us! Where are you? Josh can come and collect you."

Her sister was shaking her head. "Oh, don't worry. I've no intention of parking myself on all of you."

"Cath — it was what Dad wanted. He said as much before he left."

"Yes, maybe, but it isn't what *you* want. You've made it very clear. Don't feel bad though. I don't want it either."

"What will you do, then?"

"I'm going to do the only thing I can, the only thing I want. I'm going to find Spider and join him. He's gone north and I'm doing the same. I'm already on my way, Laura."

Laura pressed her hands into her eyes, bending her head. "But, how? How?"

"Oh, I've got my contacts. You don't live with Spider for a few years without getting to know a few people. I'll get there. And he needs me, Laura. He may not show it but he can't manage without me."

"And you're fit enough for this journey? How will you do it?"

Cath stared back at her with eyes that looked huge in her shrunken face. "You don't need to know that. It's better that you don't."

"But you'll keep in touch, won't you? How will we know you're safe? How will Jack know — and Ethan?" Laura's voice rose as she felt panic rising in her throat.

"Laura, they are both better off with you — for now. Who knows what might happen in the future? One, or both, of them may decide to join us one day. But at least with you I know they'll be safe, fed and sheltered. I'll find some way to contact you when I'm settled but I'm saying goodbye now because I have to go — OK?"

At that moment Laura wanted to wrap her arms around her sister and hug her as never before. Then she and her image were gone. She sat listless in the chair, thinking she'd need to message Josh and Ethan. But no, she'd wait to tell them in person, together with Jack, at which point he and Holly came tumbling through the door, breathless and animated from racing up the tunnel.

Longhope

He put his shoulder to the door at the top of the steps to the Submariner and pushed hard, hearing the squally wind whipping about outside. It yielded with a clang back against the building and he was subjected to the push of the angry, whistling wind as it pummelled him. Bent into it, he retraced their steps and made his way down towards the dockside.

Plumes of spray were leaping out in tall spumes and slapping down on to the paved quay in front of the warehouses. In harbour the water was a grey wash of white topped waves, ships bucking and jostling and further out, boathouses dipping and rising like panicking horses. He took a minute to look over at Futura, where she lay at mooring amongst the ships, secure, sleek and safe.

Quay warehouses stretched ahead. In the first row were well maintained corporation buildings; the harbour office, customs sheds. He forged on until he reached the next row with their own, modest unit, unlocked it and dived inside, pressing the button to close the steel door to as he scanned the shelves and pallets for something he could use. In a corner by the door there was a metal chest with rusting corners and faded writing which he knew contained tools. He pulled up the lid to scan the contents. Outside the gale continued, muffled by the closed, steel door.

In the chest there were thick ropes, bio-oil cans, chains, grappling hooks and hammers. He considered the hammers, frowning, then spotted a long, heavy spanner. He picked it up and swung it to and fro in his right hand, grunting with satisfaction at the movement of his new arm as it manipulated the weight. He placed the spanner on the concrete floor and rummaged around some more until he found a blade, part of an ancient harpoon that Hugh once used, which he tucked into his belt. He turned his attention to the remainder of the shed, searching around the stacked pallets until he spotted a coil of rope on a hook in the wall. He lifted it off and slung it over his shoulder.

Ethan stood up straight, walked to the door and waited while it slid up. Then he felt the buzz of his wrist console which was flashing.

"Ethan. Josh for you."

"Ethan, where have you got to? I'm about finished here. We should maybe think about getting back now. It's looking like the calm break is done and I'd like to get home before it gets too much worse."

He placed the spanner on the floor, removed his wrist console and closed it down. He couldn't remember a time when he'd ever done this before and felt oddly exposed, as if naked in the Wastelands. But he lost no time; he would have to get on with this before Josh came looking for him.

He stepped out into the gale and pressed the close and lock button. Towards the end of the rows, the warehouse buildings were smaller, scruffier, less well-maintained, their doors and roofs rusting. Further still there were no electronic mechanisms but the doors were secured with old-fashioned padlocks, easier to break into. He paused at the first of them, the rough door rattling, the padlock rusted. It looked unused, with no marks of recent entry. He stepped along to the next, a smaller building, once green-painted but with little paint left. The padlock was new and shiny, though Ethan didn't know where you could get such things these days. He pulled at it. The bolt came out of its housing. The door was not locked, but the padlock had been pushed together to look as if it was. He removed it and hooked it through the hinge on the side of the door, glanced around, pulled the door open a sliver and slipped inside, almost closing the door to behind him.

Once his eyes had adjusted to the dingy gloom, he saw that the interior had been used as storage. There were several free-standing sets of industrial units and shelves along two sides of the space. There was a strong smell of bio-fuel as well as an aroma of stale food. Some cartons littered the floor. A stained tarpaulin was piled in one corner. In another there was a low stack of pallets on top of which a stained mattress and some tangled blankets lay. Ethan moved over to the makeshift bed and pulled the blankets back, recoiling at the stale smell that rose from them. He stepped back and listened but could hear nothing except the continual buffeting of the wind outside as it rattled the door.

He stooped to get a closer look at the area around the pallets, moving the cartons around with the spanner, spotting some crumpled yellow paper which he reached for. As he did, a shaft of light appeared, illuminating the corner where he squatted and he stood and turned, hearing the scraping of the door as it swung open, a dark, bulky shape silhouetted, the sound of the wind a sudden roar that was cut off as the door slammed shut and the lights went on.

Porc. He stood in front of the door, a large carton under one arm, grinning. Ethan faced him, gripping the spanner.

Joshua said goodbye to Reuben and ran up the steps to the area outside the bar, wrestling the door open as Ethan had. Sheets of fine rain were now blowing across the docks, making visibility difficult. He squinted, shielding his eyes with his hand as he looked for a sign of Ethan. Why hadn't he answered his wrist console? His own wrist buzzed, where he stood at the top of the steps. Laura.

"Josh? Are you on your way? I've started dinner."

"We won't be long, love. We're just having a chat with Reuben, reminiscing. He sends his regards to you."

There was a pause. "Oh, what? You're still in the bar? You need to hurry, Josh. The storm's boiling up. Say hello to Reuben from me and wrap it up!"

"OK. We'll scoop up and get going. Bye, love."

"Josh — wait! Cath messaged."

"Cath? She is in contact? Where is she? We asked Reuben about her. He thinks she's gone to find Spider. How does she look?"

"He's right. She's on her way. She won't say where. You can see how ill she's been; she's lost a lot of weight and looks older. I tried to persuade her to come to us but she is adamant that all she wants is to be with *him,* with Spider."

"You can't do any more for her, love. We're caring for her two boys as it is." He rolled his eyes as he spoke, thinking of Ethan and how he'd no clue as to the boy's whereabouts right now.

"Look, we'll be back as soon as we can and we can talk about it then, OK?"

He cursed his son as he ran down the walkway and began making his way towards the dock.

Ethan tightened his grip on the spanner and licked his lips. The man leered from beneath his black eyebrows and stooped to place the carton on the floor beside him. His voice sounded thick and soft. "Company! Want something?"

Ethan swallowed. Porc was not afraid. If anything, he appeared delighted. He began the sentence he'd rehearsed a hundred times in his mind whenever he'd imagined this meeting. He used a voice as strong as he could muster.

"I've come to seek justice for our friend. The one

you killed at our farm."

Porc sniggered, nodding his head. "You're the young bastard nobody wanted, that got taken on there when you were crippled. Justice, eh? Why would this have anything to do with me? Why would you be breaking and entering my property? I could call the cops and get you put away." He paused. "Or I could just deal with the matter myself, couldn't I?"

"You won't call the police," Ethan said, "because that would draw their attention to you and with some help from me, they could find something that links you to the murder."

The man tilted his head back, laughing. Ethan could smell stale sweat emanating from his unwashed clothes. "That weren't no murder, son! Them dogs got him. That was an accident, see? Fair and square. Man was a fool. You don't enter any space with the dogs unless you're the handler. He should have known better, shouldn't he?" He was nodding now, pleased with his own defence. "Pressing thing is, son, what am I going to do with you, now?"

"You were there, when it happened. You were the handler. You could have called the dogs off. That makes you a murderer, whatever you say."

"Yeah? Supposing I was? There's no evidence to say I was there when it happened. None at all. But suppose I was there? Eh? What are *you* going to do about it?"

The young man raised his chin and took a step

closer. Now he was almost in reach with the spanner. He could smell his adversary's breath, sour with stale alcohol and cigarette fumes. Porc grinned, put a hand behind his back and produced a gun, a large pistol. Ethan's stomach lurched and he felt burning acid reach his throat. "You wouldn't get away with another murder, not this time."

"No? Not if it was self-defence? You broke in, remember? I was asleep. You were carrying a weapon." He jerked his large head at the spanner. There was an affirmatory click as he cocked the pistol.

At once a rasping squeal signalled the rusty door being wrenched open. The burly man made an involuntary half turn towards it, distracted. Ethan took his chance, leapt forward and struck the gun arm with his spanner then lunged at him, propelling him out through the open door and on to the paved quayside, where tall plumes of spray and waves were lashing both the paving and the buildings.

Taken unawares, Porc stumbled backwards and fell on to the wet slabs, pulling Ethan over on top of him. Having lost his grip on the gun, he got his hands around the younger man's neck and began to squeeze. They rolled together, Ethan kicking out, gouging at Porc's face in an effort to make him release his hold. Spray cascaded over them as they neared the leaping waves of the harbour, closer still to the edge, each spume drenching them, seeming to reach for them to pull them over as they wrestled. Then there was a sudden, explosive crack, the large man's hands fell from Ethan's throat and he lay still, a red stream flowing from the hole in his temple and ebbing over the edge of the paving, washed away by the waves.

Ethan rolled free and lay gasping on the streaming slabs. When he opened his eyes, his stepfather was standing over him with the pistol in his hand. He watched as the gun was jettisoned out into the sea then Joshua knelt and began pushing the dead weight of the lifeless man until the corpse tipped over and into the water, disappearing from sight.

Laura

She'd somehow managed to get the children home, start them on their learning tasks and begin dinner preparation without displaying too much of the anxiety that gnawed at her. She nodded as Holly prattled about the tomato picker and argued with Jack about which tunnel was next for harvesting and was non-committal when her daughter tried to enlist her for back-up.

She stood at the window as the chem-chicken casserole simmered on the stove, frowning through at the glowering sky and horizontal mizzle engulfing the apple tree. 'Come *on'*, she whispered, willing them to get back as strong gusts hammered the eaves and bent over what remained of the hedge around Hugh's garden.

She was setting the table when the children came in, first Holly then Jack. Though it always seemed as if she led him around Laura knew this was not always the case. Jack was his own man now, curious, independent, intelligent, giving as good as he got from her feisty young daughter.

"Mum, when's dinner? I'm starving!"

Laura continued laying places at the table. "I was hoping your Dad and Ethan would be back by now and we could all eat together."

"They should hurry. It's boiling up! Can we have a snack while we're waiting?"

Laura chewed her lip, brow knitted. "Tell you what, why don't you go and see if Ewa is ready to eat and she, Jack and you can all have your dinner now. They can eat when they get back."

Holly darted out in the direction of Ewa's quarters. Jack stayed, leaning against the counter, arms folded, eyeing Laura. "What's holding them up?" he asked. She went to the stove, took a ladle and stirred the casserole, her back to him.

"Oh — they got talking with Reuben at the bar, remembering old times. We should all go down and see him one day, Jack. I expect he'd love to see you again."

Jack was still, watching her. "They would know better than to hang around chatting when the weather is worsening. Something must be up. Maybe the van is mal-functioning?"

Laura turned around, fixing a smile. "No. Nothing's wrong. I messaged Joshua and he just forgot the time. They'll be here in a minute. If there was a problem, they'd let us know!"

The boy continued to scrutinise her. "Why don't you message again?"

He was right. She knew she must do it. But not here, not in front of him. "Here," she said. "Stir this a moment while I speak to Josh."

In the study she sat on the window seat where she'd see if the van appeared. The storm had strengthened, rain lashing the glass and wind buffeting the roof. "PAM. Please try Joshua for me."

His image appeared. He was inside, somewhere dark. It looked as if Ethan was behind him, seated. "Josh! What's going on? Why haven't you started back?"

"Love," his voice sounded strange, constricted, "we've left it too late to set off now. We'll have to stay over."

"It's not like you!" she cried. "What's happened? Where — where will you stay? With Reuben?"

He shook his head. "No. Reuben only has a cupboard, Laura. We're going to sleep on the boat tonight; on Futura. Don't worry about us. We'll be fine. But don't tell anyone where we are — not the children or anyone else. Just say we're staying in Longhope tonight, OK? We don't want to worry them."

Behind his stepfather, Ethan was getting to his feet. She saw Josh put a protective arm around her son. Ethan's face was pale, his shoulders hunched. He was holding his jacket together around his neck as though he was cold. When he spoke, his voice was hoarse and cracked as if it pained him. He smiled weakly. "Hi Laura. We are fine, please don't worry about us! Can you get Ewa to message me? I need to ask her something."

Laura shut her console down and went to the kitchen, where Jack, Ewa and Holly were seated at the table, Kav on Holly's lap banging a spoon and crowing

263

with glee. As Laura entered the room, she could see Jack's eyes following her, questioning.

She picked up a cloth and began to wipe a work surface, avoiding their searching looks. "They're staying over in town tonight. They got delayed and the weather is too bad to set off. They're staying with Reuben at the Sub."

The three stared at her. Kav ceased banging and attempted to rekindle Holly's interest by pulling her nose.

"Ewa, Ethan wants you to message him." Laura turned to them, her face white, her voice flat.

Ewa rose, startled, and left the room.

Ethan and Ewa

Ewa sat down in her living room, her heart thumping, her palms wet. After a moment Ethan floated in front of her, seated on some kind of platform covered with rags, the space around him dark. Joshua was nowhere to be seen.

"Ethan, are you OK? Laura said you won't be back tonight."

He was smiling, but one hand held the collar of his coat together as if he was cold.

"Are you sick?" she asked.

He cleared his throat. "I'm all right. Listen, I want to ask you something. Something serious. I'll need to know your answer tonight."

Ewa swallowed. "What is it?"

"Ewa, I'm going back to sea. Don't say anything to Laura yet. We're staying on the boat tonight and Josh is coming back tomorrow but I won't be with him. You've heard me say it often enough, that I don't want to be a farmer; I never wanted to work on the land. Laura will be unhappy when she finds out but she'll understand when she thinks about it. I want you to come with me, you and Kav. Will you? I have to know tonight because I'll be sailing tomorrow whatever happens with the storm."

She stared, aghast, stammering. "I — I don't know. Why must it be so sudden? I know we've talked about it a little, but there would be much to do. We would have to prepare. And what about your family? You are needed here, more than ever, at the farm. And there is Kav. I thought we were waiting until he is a little older to decide."

He gazed at her, his eyes ablaze, pleading. "Ewa, please trust me. There is a reason I must go tomorrow. I'll explain when you are here but you must decide now and then you'll have to pack for yourself and for Kav, just the minimum that you both need, your personal stuff, warm clothing, waterproofs. Josh will take care of explaining to the others."

"Something has happened, Ethan. What is it? Why can't you tell me?"

"I'll let you know when you are here with me, Ewa. You have to trust me. Please. I love you and I love Kav. You know that. I want us to be together, always."

She stared down at her lap, twisting her hands together, her blue eyes misty. To leave with him, to put to sea, it was a step into the unknown; it was a step away from her life to date, her memories, her time with Farlow. And he was here, would be here for ever — except that he wasn't. Farlow was gone. He existed now only in her memory and in the legacy of his son, Kav. She gathered herself, staring up at Ethan with an intense gaze. "We'll come. I'll get our things together.

Whatever has happened, Ethan, we are in it together. We belong together. I will be with you and so will Kav. But I will have to tell them: Laura, Holly and Jack."

"Yes. And they'll try to stop you, try to stop *us*. You have to be strong, though. I'll see you tomorrow. And we'll never be separated again. Remember."

She nodded. "We'll be there."

He was gone. She stood up, raised her chin and walked through to the kitchen.

The Leaving

It was a solemn group that assembled next morning on the wharf next to where Futura lay docked. The vessel bobbed up and down on the restraining ropes as if eager to be away. Further out in the bay, remnants of float-homes dotted the water, most now abandoned or taken over by opportunistic squatters. Holly took a moment to peer through the mizzle at the remains of Nell's family's home, a forlorn, roofless hulk now, looted and vandalised; even the high-tech, weather-proof material covering the walls and deck had been pilfered. Holly had tried to discover the whereabouts of her best friend, but Mrs Philips was a victim of the disease and, as yet, nobody had seen fit to replace her, or the distance learning system that she operated. While Holly and Jack, like many other survivor pupils, were being home-tutored, many others were neglected, a generation growing up with no education at all.

Joshua, who'd arrived home before dawn, had tried hard to exclude Laura and the children from the departure, telling them it was risky to all of them, especially to Ethan. But Laura, once she'd come to accept that the three were going, was not to be deterred from seeing them off. Holly had also insisted she be there. "Ethan is my brother and Kav is my nephew," she'd said, and though this was not strictly accurate, nobody had the heart to correct her. Jack came along because he was part of them now and it was beyond anyone to leave him behind. On the bumpy, squashed ride down to Longhope he'd made a silent, fervent wish to be able to see all of Futura and inspect her advanced navigational system.

In the end it had been easier than Ewa had imagined, to say they'd be leaving. Laura had reacted with a dignified, dry-eyed nod to the inevitable and it had been left to Holly to leap up, stricken and red-faced and run from the room, upstairs to her bed, where she flung herself, howling. Jack remained, impassive, while Laura spoke to Ewa in a calm, measured tone.

"Ewa, it's not unexpected. But it is sudden. I thought, after Hugh went and now Cath, that we'd all have more time together, that we'd be able to be a proper family for a while, here in this house. You are my daughter now, as much as Ethan is my son and Kav my grandson. I'm worried that you are not ready, that you won't be safe. You've had no experience of the sea, which is becoming more unpredictable and dangerous as time goes on."

Ewa nodded. "Yes, but Ethan is experienced and he is a natural, talented mariner. He will teach me. It will be hard for us, Kav and me, and we may be sick, at first. But Ethan will keep us safe, I know he will. Something bad has happened. Ethan needs to get away, sooner than he wanted to. I trust him, Laura. We will always be able to message. It won't be like it is with your sister!"

"I know. And I'm sure Ethan will do everything he can to protect you both. It's just that the seas have become so wild, so stormy now! And yes, we can message but it isn't the same as hugging and talking face-to-face." She paused. Just when she'd been getting used to having Ethan around, he was leaving again, in some circumstances she didn't understand. She glanced at Jack, who sat at the table, seeming not to listen, fidgeting with a console he'd removed from his wrist. She was losing Ethan and had gained Jack. For a moment it seemed a gross injustice, to have this difficult, diffident child as a replacement for her brilliant, loving son. This must be how small, parent birds used to feel when they were obliged to raise an infant cuckoo. But she was being unfair, she knew. Nothing was for ever. Whatever had happened she must support the decision.

"Let's sit down and eat," she said. "Then I'll help you to pack. We'll put our heads together to find the most useful items for you both."

Ewa smiled her gratitude. Laura was not about to make their departure more difficult than it already was. The wailing from upstairs had stopped. Laura served the meal. "I'm just going to see if Holly is feeling like eating."

The girl lay silent as Laura entered and sat on the edge of the bed, stroking her hair. "You're feeling

270

terrible and I feel the same, love, but how you feel right now isn't going to change what will happen. You can choose, though. You can either stay here, feeling bad or you can wash your face, come down and eat and look after Kav while Ewa and I get their things ready."

Holly turned and sat up, her face blotchy, hair wild. Laura hugged her.

They'd packed Ewa and Kav's luggage into produce cartons so that when they unloaded the vehicle the impression was of a freight consignment. The children also took a carton each which allowed them access to Futura without arousing suspicion. The difficulty was getting the baby on board, a problem which Joshua solved by placing him also into a box for his mother to carry up the gangway. This enraged Kav, whose muffled wails were audible to those nearby but could not be detected by onlookers above the lament of the gale or the sloshing of choppy waves.

At last they were all gathered, squeezed into Futura's tiny salon. Ewa scooped Kav out of the box and he crowed with delight, easing the tension and making everyone smile as she passed him to Holly and stepped towards Ethan, who drew her to him.

Laura thought Ethan looked exhausted. If anything, he seemed more drained than he'd been after the accident. But he was sporting a wan smile as he put an arm around his girl's waist and addressed his family. "I'm grateful to you all. I'm going to leave it to Josh to explain what has happened to you. When we are underway and under sail, I'm going to do the same for Ewa. For now, though, it's enough to say I am a fugitive. I've done something I think was right but the law will judge as wrong. I wanted to stay and face justice. We talked it over, Josh and I, all night. Now he's talked me out of it and I'm running away — sailing away." He pulled Ewa closer. "We'll be away a while but we will come back to visit as soon as everything has settled down. I promise!"

Holly sat down on the bench seat with Kav, hugging him close and making him squawk as he tried to pull her hair. Her face felt hot as she glanced around at the others, her mother pale, her father sombre, Jack's eyes alight with interest as he concentrated.

Joshua rallied. His rangy frame was bent to fit under the roof of the vessel's modest salon. "Right, Ethan, it's about time you got underway, before the tide turns and the port workers start their morning shift."

"Message us as soon as you can, once you're away and clear!" Laura fought her distress, biting her lip until she drew blood.

It was the moment they were all dreading. They stepped forward in turn to hug, all except for Jack and Kav, shedding more tears. "Look business-like when you leave the ship," warned Josh. "We mustn't make it look like we've been saying goodbye or that we're upset. We've simply been loading our goods on to a transport vessel."

As they filed back across to the jetty the sound of

Futura's engine purring into life was just audible above the wailing wind. Josh and Laura removed the cumbersome gangplank with its handrails then moved to the bollards to unwind the heavy ropes that bound her to the shore. Through the driving rain, Kav's round, chubby, laughing face could be seen in the porthole, Ewa holding his hand to make him wave. A watery gap appeared between the ship and the dock side as she slid away. Ethan's tousled head appeared briefly and he raised a hand before ducking back inside to manoeuvre the prow around and towards the harbour gap.

"Into the van!" Josh ordered them, fearful as the three stood transfixed. They bundled in, he started the engine and they rolled towards Longhope, each silent.

Meanwhile on a gantry attached to the harbour floodlight, the small surveillance camera swivelled to turn its prying eye upon them and follow their progress up into the almost deserted village.

Aftermath

They have clambered up to a high ledge, near enough to hear the turbines' roar and to make out Longhope, far below and only just visible through the drifting mizzle. They are insulated against the driving rain and blustery wind, zipped into parkas and waterproof trousers.

Holly has been quiet these last few weeks, prone to long, contemplative silences and less argumentative. At first Jack preferred her this way, less bossy, less opinionated and less knowing but now, though he wouldn't admit to it, he misses their old skirmishes and her habit of telling him what to do.

Perching on a wet rock, he pulls two apples from his pocket. "Want one?"

She shakes her head, still staring out at where the horizon might be. "He'll be OK, your brother. He'll bring them back, too, Ewa and the baby. When it's all died down. He's cool, I reckon."

She turns on him. "He can't come back; not after the accident. Dad said. Everyone will think he was responsible because he left in a hurry!" Holly is flushed. These days she is prone to mood swings, emotional turmoil wrought from recent events and in part due to adolescent hormones.

Jack finishes his apple and lobs the core into a clump of rapeseed. "Whatever. You believe that, then?"

"What?"

"You believe it was an accident."

"Of course. That's what my Dad said, wasn't it?"

He shakes his head. "It's what your Dad wants us to believe."

Holly can feel a hot well of fury bubbling up inside her. "Go on then. Say what *you* think happened."

The boy glances at her, shrugging. "Your brother went down there to the docks and killed him. End of."

"He wouldn't. Ethan wouldn't kill anyone. You don't know him like I do!"

Jack stands up, dark, wet strands of unruly hair plastered to his face. "True. I can see why he'd want to, though. The guy was a creep."

When she turns her back on him and stomps away down the muddy track, he rolls his eyes and follows her.

Miles away, across the seas, Futura rests at anchor in a sheltered cove. Her hold is full of textile bales for recycling. Inside the compact cabin, Ewa places a sleeping Kav into his baby hammock before climbing the stairs to the deck. Ethan, swathed in waterproofs is making secure and battening down.

They stand together, silent, looking out to sea.

"What I did…" Ethan begins.

She places a finger to his lips. "Ethan, you've told me the truth. That is all that matters. I know what you did and why you did it. The man was a murderer who was never going to be brought to justice."

He tightens his arm around her shoulders. "You have to understand that I didn't go down there to kill him. I wanted to make him confess and to bring him in to face up to his crime. Nobody else was going to do it. What happened — it didn't turn out like I meant it to."

For a few minutes they stay here on deck, watching as the last of the light dwindles in the west.

"Is this going to be enough for the pair of you, do you think? It may be too much to expect that you can give up your life at the farm and your surrogate family to be on this small craft with only myself for company. It will be hard. And it will be lonely at times."

She shakes her head. "Ethan…"

"I want you to promise me, Ewa. Promise that you'll tell me if you change your mind, if you decide that sea life, or life with me, or both, are not what you want. Then I'll be down, but I'll understand. The life is not for everyone. And it will be tricky bringing up a child on board. There'll be safety issues and there isn't a lot of room."

She faces him. "I'll promise. But it won't happen. The trading will be much better with two of us. I may not be much use yet with the sailing although I can learn. But I know a lot about making contacts and about running a business. We can make this work, Ethan. I want to. I want us to be together, with Kav. We loved Farlow and I won't allow his memory to fade but you are like a father to my child now. He will grow up into this life, will live his whole life at sea and will know nothing different. We belong together, the three of us. This is the promise I will make."

He hugs her. The light has gone from the sky and all that remains is the mast light, casting a soft, pale line across the water; wavering, breaking up but staying true until tomorrow comes.